# DARK IS THE MORNING

# DARK IS THE MORNING

## RUPERT THOMSON

OTHER PRESS | NEW YORK

Production editor: Yvonne E. Cárdenas
Text designer: Chris Welch
This book was set in Bembo Std by
Alpha Design & Composition of Pittsfield, NH

10 9 8 7 6 5 4 3 2 1



Library of Congress Cataloging-in-Publication Data
Names: Thomson, Rupert author
Title: Dark is the morning : a novel / Rupert Thomson.
Description: New York : Other Press, 2026.
Identifiers: LCCN 2025044780 (print) | LCCN 00024411447 (ebook) |
    ISBN 9781635422283 paperback | ISBN 9781635422290 ebook
Subjects: LCGFT: Novels | Fiction | Romance fiction
Classification: LCC PR6070.H685 D36 2026  (print) |
    LCC PR6070.H685 (ebook)
LC record available at https://lccn.loc.gov/2025044780
LC ebook record available at https://lccn.loc.gov/2025044781

Publisher's Note: This is a work of fiction. Names, characters, places,
and incidents either are the product of the author's imagination or are
used fictitiously, and any resemblance to actual persons, living or dead,
events, or locales is entirely coincidental.

Then I die with anxiety, then my wild mind imagines
who embraces my love, and in what ways:
then I call curses down
        —TIBULLUS


Dark is the morning that passes
without the light of your eyes
        —CESARE PAVESE

# I.
# HARRY

THERE IS A house in Abruzzo, on the steep but fertile slope between the ancient hilltop town of Vasto and the Adriatic Sea. Its walls are charred and blackened, and several of the windows have lost their glass. A sign that says BEWARE OF THE DOG hangs on the metal fence that surrounds the property, but the dog in question has long gone—if indeed there ever was a dog. The lawn has not been cut in years, and one of the huge terra-cotta urns has fallen over. The pool is empty.

To live in that beautiful place, among the olive groves, the acacia trees, and the bursts of pink and dark red oleander, you need to be wealthy. Many of the houses are recent builds, not farmhouses, but villas and haciendas, with wide sun terraces, lawn sprinklers, and electric gates. The peaceful, almost sleepy one-lane roads and the views over the wide blue sweep of the Adriatic give the area an exclusive feel.

Hardly anyone passes through, just residents, and the occasional cyclist in bright, tight-fitting Lycra.

Only the other day, I took a left turn off Via Istonia and drove up to the house. I stopped by the front gate and put the car in neutral. It was a pilgrimage of sorts—or perhaps I was trying, once again, to come to terms with what happened back in the early 2000s.

I still find the whole thing hard to believe.

# II.

# GINO

IT HAD ALL started so well. I was surprised that Raul had included me in his birthday celebrations, since I had only been working in the department for a few months. Raul was my boss. Eighteen of us gathered on Thursday evening, in his favorite restaurant in Vasto, but then, towards midnight, as the other guests were beginning to take their leave, I ran into Uccello, an acquaintance from my teenage years, and suddenly I found myself in a basement club, drinking rum and Coke and doing lines of God knows what.

I glanced at my watch. Twenty to seven.

As the road curved uphill, through the woods, I shifted into second gear. My heart was leaping in my chest, and my mouth tasted of ash. I must have smoked about a thousand cigarettes. The sky soared overhead, its pale blue dusted with gold, though the sun hadn't lifted above the mountains yet, and the olive groves and vineyards in the valley were still in shadow. Somehow, it was Friday already. Where had Thursday gone?

I passed the track that led to the six-hundred-year-old oak tree, then I rounded the final bend, and there was Caracciolo, its houses arranged along the spine of a ridge, facades of bare concrete and decaying stone, most of them austere, untended, the church taller than the rest.

Caracciolo, where I had been born and raised.

I would die there too, if I wasn't careful.

When I walked into the kitchen, my father was sitting at the table, dressed in a blue shirt and a gray waistcoat. He liked to help out at the *comune*, in an administrative role. In his fifties and early sixties, he had served two terms as mayor of the village, and he had kept in touch with things ever since, even though he was past retirement age. Once he stopped work, he would probably spend all his time on the land, growing the fruit and vegetables he was famous for. As I pulled up outside the house, I had known that he would be waiting for me. He was always there when I fell. Not to catch me, though. No, never that.

I thought it was a dinner, he said. His head was lowered, and he was turning his empty coffee cup on its saucer.

It was, I said. But then I ran into somebody I used to know, and one thing led to another.

All this running around. It's making your mother unhappy.

He looked at me, over his shoulder. His eyes were dark brown and soulful, just like mine. It was something that people who knew our family would come out with—*You've got your father's eyes*—though it was always said with a certain regret, as if they weren't actually talking about similarities at all, but about differences, the things I hadn't managed to inherit from my father. His judgment, his patience. His goodness.

You'll be thirty soon, he said. Perhaps it's time to think about settling down.

I couldn't help laughing.

People don't do that anymore, I said. And anyway, I'm nowhere near thirty.

My father ran a hand over his thinning hair, not quite touching it. What happened to Franca?

Franca?

Marcello's daughter. You used to like her.

Why are you talking about Franca all of a sudden? I haven't seen her for years.

She wanted to marry you, didn't she?

For Christ's sake, Dad, not you as well. It was bad enough hearing that from all my friends.

My father looked down again, the corners of his

mouth twitching. He had this way of smiling that looked painful.

I'm just saying. Standing up, he took his cup over to the sink and gave it a quick rinse. I think she's living in San Salvo now.

He placed the cup in the drying rack, then picked up his keys and walked towards the door, resting a hand on my shoulder for a moment as he passed me.

When he had left the house, I climbed the stairs. Pausing outside my parents' bedroom, I heard a murmur. That was my mother, Gabriella, saying her rosary. I moved on down the passageway. Once in my room, I closed the shutters against the daylight, then I lay down on my bed.

Franca.

She had appeared in class when I was nine. I don't know where she had been to school before. Maybe in Gissi, which was where her family were from. Or maybe nowhere. She was a strange, stringy little thing, with a thin face and brown hair that hung past her shoulders. People were cruel to her at the beginning, especially the girls. They called her The Rat. It didn't seem to bother her too much. She'd probably been called names before. Either that, or she didn't care what people thought.

About three weeks after she arrived, she walked up to me at break. I was sitting in the corner of the playground, near the war memorial, reading a comic. My friend Luca wasn't far away. One day, Gino, she said, I'm going to marry you. I don't remember how I reacted. I expect I was embarrassed. I might even have said something cheap and spiteful like, Why on earth would I agree to that? At the time, my nickname was Dopey, after the dwarf in Snow White, not because I didn't talk or because I had big ears, but because my expression was the same as his. So people thought. After Franca's declaration, Luca and the others were always on at me. *Dopey and The Rat, Dopey and The Rat.* I heard it all the time. So Dopey, they'd say, when's the wedding? And, What if the Pied Piper shows up? And, If you have a baby, it's definitely going to have a tail. For the next few years, I avoided Franca. Sometimes I felt her eyes on me in class, or in the playground, but she didn't approach me again. Gradually, she made friends among the girls.

The next time I spoke to her was Halloween. I would have been about thirteen. A rumor had gone round that something was happening in the tall brick house at the top end of the village. The house belonged to an Englishman called Harry French. Bald with black eyebrows, Harry had the rounded shoulders and thick wrists of a wrestler, but he worked in Hong Kong, my father told me, as a market trader. He was one of the first foreigners to buy a property in the village. My father helped him with the paperwork, and also with the renovations, and the two men became friends. I called Harry *Il Francese*—The Frenchman—though not to his face.

That evening, as the sun went down, a group of us walked over to the house. It was almost dark, but no lights showed in the windows. A pumpkin stood on a stone pedestal outside. From inside the house came thin violin music and sinister rumblings. Every now and then there was a blood-chilling scream.

As we watched, the door creaked open, seemingly of its own accord. On a chair in the hallway sat a figure dressed in black. His face was painted white, and blood trickled from his mouth. Behind him, on a table, three candles flickered in a silver candelabra. The door slammed abruptly, without him even lifting a finger.

Luca gave me a nudge. Your wife's over there.

I looked where he was looking. A little further down the hill, Franca was standing beneath a streetlamp with some other girls.

Don't be boring, I said.

Luca grinned, then shrugged.

The door creaked open again. This time there was a bowl of sweets on the tiled floor, halfway between the man's chair and the door. When one of the small boys edged forwards, asking if he could have a sweet, a gorilla leapt from the shadows. The boy fled, screaming. The beast lumbered after him, beating its chest and roaring. The vampire in the chair tipped his head back and laughed, revealing a set of jagged, bloodstained teeth. Some of the younger children were crying. Others would have nightmares for weeks afterwards.

After about an hour, the sound effects inside the house cut out, and the door remained closed. Luca and his cronies drifted off into the night. When I looked round, Franca was still over by the streetlamp. She was on her own.

Looks like it's finished, I said, turning away.

She asked if I was going home.

I said I was.

A light rain had begun to fall. I tilted my head skywards and felt tiny specks of water landing on my face.

She moved closer. You mind if I walk with you?

I didn't say yes. But I didn't say no either.

She lived not far from me, in a new apartment block near the sports ground, but instead of turning left up the main street, which would have taken us home in a matter of minutes, we walked down the hill as far as the medieval fountain, then round the back of the school and up the steep steps next to the post office.

It was pretty good, don't you think? she said.

You weren't scared?

No, not really.

Me neither.

It felt like Dracula was real, she said, and he was in our village. She paused. And King Kong.

I liked her take on things—how she managed to give praise while remaining cool and jaded. I liked the way her hair hung past her shoulders, almost to her waist. One of her front teeth had a small piece missing. She had run into a door when she was eight, she told me. Blood everywhere. Luckily, her father was an ambulance driver. I laughed. She didn't have any sweets of her own. I gave her some of mine.

When we reached the top of the steps, where she would turn left, and I would go straight on, she asked if I knew about the convent at the head of the valley. Apparently, it had once been used as a cocaine factory. She had heard her father talking about it on the phone.

She glanced at me, and her pupils seemed to flare. You think we should investigate?

We met a few days later, on the road that led out of the village. It was late afternoon. November. The air smelled of woodsmoke and dead leaves. Though the convent was close by, it was down in the valley, and hidden by the trees. Once in a while, on Sundays, the church was used for mass, but the convent buildings were abandoned. As we walked, I told her that I would be going to school in Vasto the following year. I wanted her to be excited for me, but she didn't say anything. She didn't even look at me.

I'll be back in the evenings, I said, and at weekends.

You'll make new friends. Her head was lowered, and her hands were pushed deep into the pockets of her jeans. You'll have a different life.

I realized I had to do something to change the mood. Let's run, I said.

I didn't know where the idea had come from, but when I set off she kept pace with me.

We had only been running for a few seconds when I began to laugh. Soon we were both laughing. I wasn't sure why. Perhaps because running was something we never did, not if we could help it. Neither of us were any good at sport.

We stopped under the trees where the road curved sharply. We were panting. I had a stitch.

Kiss me, she said.

She was standing close to me, her face in shadow. I looked at her, but didn't move. I couldn't. Leaves stirred overhead.

You don't want to, she said. You think I'm ugly.

It's not that, I said.

Is it because I'm from Gissi?

In Caracciolo, we tended to look down on anyone from Gissi. My uncle, Pasquale, always said that the only reason to go to Gissi was to take a piss. His father used to say the same thing. As for me, I didn't understand what the problem was.

I shook my head. No.

What, then?

I looked at the ground. I don't know.

Fuck. She stared off into the trees. You idiot. She was talking to herself. I'm sorry, she said. Forget it.

It was the first time I had heard her swear. She kept surprising me in ways that made me think I should be interested in her.

We started walking.

When we reached the convent, it was in darkness. From further down the valley came the sound of barking. There was an old woman who lived on a farm all by herself. She had more than a dozen dogs, if the rumors were to be believed.

On the far side of the building, where the undergrowth was at its most dense and tangled, we found a door that was secured by nothing other than a piece of twisted wire. The door opened into a storeroom. There was a wooden ladder propped against the wall and a floor of beaten earth. Some demijohns stood in the corner, their green glass furred with dust. Speaking in whispers, we moved on through the building. In a room on the first floor, on a table, we discovered traces of white powder. We looked at each other. Was this the evidence we were after? Rolling a page torn from an old prayer book, I snorted some of the powder. My nostril burned, and I began to sneeze. Franca touched a finger to the powder and rubbed it on her teeth and gums, then she spat quickly. That's chalk, she said, or plaster. I stared at her. Where did you learn how to do that? She was nonchalant, as always. I must have seen it in a movie.

Though its days as a cocaine factory were long gone, if indeed anything like that had ever happened, the convent became our headquarters. We set up camp in a room with a vaulted ceiling and a window that looked over the valley. We'd bring a bottle of wine with us, and some rolling tobacco, and a candle, and we'd sit at the table by the window and pretend we were in a bar. Even weeks later, the words that had caught me off guard—*Kiss me*—still hung in the air, not like a regret, not even like a possibility, but like a covenant that bound us together. Sometimes Franca would tease me, slanting her eyes towards some flakes of whitewash. *Fancy a line?* Oddly, I would feel approved of. She had chosen not to see my snorting of some ordinary dust as a reason to mock me, but as something exuberant or cavalier, something that helped to color in the legend of ourselves that we were already in the process of creating. Perhaps that was why I felt able to start talking about my father.

Nothing I do is ever good enough, I said.

She watched me carefully, her roll-up held close to her lips.

I seem to let him down, I said, over and over.

That's hardly a surprise, she said.

I stared at her. Rather than try to contradict me or reassure me, as others would have done, she had agreed with me.

When he was young, she said, he was some kind of hero, wasn't he?

I nodded gloomily. He foiled a fascist plot in Rome. It was in the seventies.

Leaning forwards, she placed her half-smoked roll-up on the paint-tin lid we used as an ashtray. Giancarlo Albanese, she said. He's loved by everybody in the village. He's always helping people out. He's like the salt of the earth. She gave the last phrase a peculiar emphasis, at once admiring and sarcastic. Also, he grows the best tomatoes—and not just tomatoes either. He grows the best everything. How are you going to compete with all that? You're only human.

Sometimes, when I bite into one of his tomatoes, I said, I feel like I'm going to choke on it.

She nodded. They're too perfect.

If only one of them would taste of nothing for a change. I smiled bitterly, then turned to the window and flicked my cigarette butt through the wire mesh.

When I turned back again, Franca was looking at me with an expression that was tense and direct. Slowly, she took off the gray fleece she wore, the one that said NEW YORK on the front in white letters, and then she took off the T-shirt she was wearing underneath. She wasn't wearing a bra. Reaching for her roll-up, she lit it with the lighter, then she leaned back in her chair.

What do you think? she said.

I couldn't risk speaking. I doubted that my voice would work.

Still looking at me steadily, she took a drag on her cigarette, then picked up the wine bottle by the neck and drank from it.

Do you like them?

The flame on the candle was tall and thin, and black smoke rose towards the vaulted ceiling, like a straight line drawn in charcoal.

No one's seen them before, she said. You're the first.

She finished her cigarette, and then, without any haste, and quite matter-of-factly, she put her T-shirt and her fleece back on.

As we walked back to the village that night, she told me that her relationship with her father wasn't exactly easy either. I think he wanted a daughter who was beautiful, she said. Like the women in the shows he watches on TV.

I murmured a few consoling words.

You and me, she said, it seems like we're both kind of disappointing. She stopped on the road, one side of her thin face silvered by the moon. But maybe we could be something different—to each other.

To even think of an idea like that. To be able to open up a whole new world with one short sentence. I didn't pay enough attention, though. When autumn came,

I went off to Vasto, as arranged. Franca attended the secondary school in Gissi, where her parents had both been educated, and we grew apart, just as she had predicted. At my new school, I fell in with a bad crowd. They were older than me, and they knew people who were older still, already in their twenties. They had nicknames like Toxic and Razor. Uccello was one of them. After I was expelled, I worked in dead-end jobs. I was out all night, drinking—and there was ecstasy and coke, of course. This was the nineties. I slept on other people's sofas, if I slept at all. My parents hardly saw me. Later, when I looked back, I glimpsed moments that seemed heightened or intense, like recaps in a TV drama—stealing vodka from Conad for a dare, crashing my dirt bike on the Vasto flyover, blacking out at a warehouse rave and waking up in hospital—but there were also parts of my life that weren't accounted for, long periods of blankness. Things got so out of hand that I was remanded to a psychiatric unit, then sent to a religious community in the north. I couldn't believe where I had ended up. The place didn't just treat addicts. It was a refuge for criminals and psychopaths as well, people who had been in mental institutions or in prison. I remember sitting at the breakfast table with my head lowered, trying not to make eye contact with anyone. After a year, I managed to discharge myself. I borrowed money from a friend and backpacked round Southeast Asia. When I returned, aged twenty-two, my father said I could live at home, but only if I found a job. I worked in a supermarket, stacking shelves, then at a garage. I worked night shifts in a plastics factory. Nothing seemed to last. I took off again, this time to South America. Does travel really broaden the mind? I'm not so sure. For me, it was more like anesthetic. In the early 2000s, I found myself on a flight back to Italy. By then, I had forgotten that Franca even existed. My determination to obliterate myself had been so comprehensive that she had been obliterated too. But as I lay there on that summer morning, in my parents' house, that felt like a waste. *Maybe we could be something different—to each other.* Those words resurfaced. Suddenly I didn't understand what I'd been doing for the last ten years.

I looked at my watch. Eight thirty.

Had I slept at all?

Sitting up, I put my feet on the floor and rubbed my face. I would have a shower, throw some clean clothes on.

I was due in the office in an hour.

After talking to one of Franca's cousins who lived in the village, I learned that she had a job at a small company that sold motor insurance. The following week, as I drove into Vasto in my father's car—my old red Lancia had broken down again—I invented an emergency doctor's appointment, which allowed me to leave work at four in the afternoon. By half past four I was in San Salvo. I parked outside a shabby building on a tree-lined street and sat still for a few moments, my hands gripping the steering wheel. Was I trying once again to please my father, who remained so adamantly un-impressed by my behavior, or did I feel, in some hid-den recess of my mind, that he had a point, and that Franca had been good for me? I didn't know. When I opened the car door, though, I felt lightheaded, almost giddy, like someone at high altitude.

Franca was sitting at a counter, behind a Perspex screen. She was studying the document in front of her. A middle-aged man in a gray suit sat in the back, at right angles to her, against a blue wall. The office smelled of printer ink and bitter coffee.

Franca, I said.

She lifted her eyes to mine.

She had the same narrow face, the same lank hair. In the stark, fluorescent light, her skin seemed more colorless than I remembered. But all of that, oddly, made me happy. No one else could see beyond it or beneath it to the real her.

Gino, she said, what are you doing here?

I could have asked her the same thing. She was wear-ing a tight-fitting top with sleeves that stopped short of her elbows. Horizontal stripes of purple, cream, and brown. She looked as if she belonged in an office that sold motor insurance, and yet I knew she didn't. She was like someone in disguise or under cover.

Are you free tomorrow night? I said.

She blinked, but didn't answer.

I'd like to take you out to dinner. I put the card from the restaurant I had chosen on the counter. I booked a table for nine o'clock.

She took the card. I don't think I know this place.

The owner has a gravelly voice, like someone in a gangster film. I bent a little closer to the screen. They say he's got three testicles.

Her laughter was explosive, almost like a sneeze.

The man in the suit appeared at her shoulder. Is there a problem?

Not at all, sir. This young woman has been very helpful. She's a real credit to your company.

The following night, I arrived at the restaurant a few minutes early. It was in San Salvo Marina, one or two blocks back from the sea. The owner, Giacomo, leaned in the doorway, smoking a cigarette. His orange polo shirt and yellow trousers made his quiff of silver hair look mauve.

You should have warned me, I said. I'd have worn my sunglasses.

He laughed. Anybody joining you?

Franca's coming, I told him. She's an old friend.

He looked beyond me. Is that her now?

I turned and saw Franca walking towards us across the dusty, dimly lit piazza. She was wearing a short skirt and a striped top similar to the one she'd worn at work the day before. Her legs were bare.

I introduced her to Giacomo, then he led us to the outdoor table I had reserved.

How about starting with one of my expertly crafted cocktails? he said when we were seated.

I'd love that, Franca said.

Giacomo turned to me. Not like you, he said, to be out with someone who's got a bit of class.

When he had stepped back inside, Franca leaned towards me and spoke in a whisper. Is it true about the testicles?

I shrugged. It's what they say.

I don't think I've ever heard a voice that deep.

*How about starting with one of my expertly crafted cocktails?* I was trying to imitate Giacomo.

She shook her head. Not even close.

Once our drinks had arrived, she asked what I was doing these days. I told her that I was living at home while I sorted myself out. I had a job at Lidl, in the IT department.

I think you're probably better than that. She lit a cigarette and blew the smoke into the dark. I mean, there's nothing wrong with IT—or with Lidl, for that matter. It's just, you're capable of more.

I smiled, but said nothing.

Not that I can talk, she said, working in that stupid insurance place.

We ordered an antipasto of prawns, followed by Giacomo's speciality—spaghetti marinara—and a chilled bottle of trebbiano.

Over our main course, I asked Franca whether she was seeing anybody. She leaned back in her chair, one hand resting on the table. Her eyes were steady. There, once again, was the unlikely confidence that I remembered from when we were young. She could be a getaway driver, I thought. She didn't panic easily, and she knew how to pass unnoticed. This anonymity was deceptive, though. It wasn't the whole story. Her real life happened in the discrepancy between her outward appearance and her inner spirit, but I was beginning to suspect that, for me, they were one and the same.

I went out with a married man for a while, she said. He was older.

Not from the village?

I'm not an idiot.

I grinned. What happened?

I had to end it. She drank from her glass, then put it back on the table. We used to meet in hotels on the Adriatica. The Sabrina, the Nettuno. The Venezia. We didn't use our real names. We had to be careful. But he was always looking over his shoulder, as if he was worried he was being followed. The first few times, he couldn't get it up. She looked away into the darkness of the piazza. When I told him it was over, he turned nasty. He said I was lucky to have been with him. I didn't know how lucky I was. He didn't stop there either. He said I wouldn't find anybody else. I'd be alone—maybe forever. She lit another cigarette. I think he wanted me to start crying or get down on my knees and beg. I laughed at him instead. You think I'm scared of that? I said. I never loved you. I just wanted the sex—and the sex, to be honest, wasn't all that great. I won't be missing much. That was when he sort of bared his teeth. For a moment, I felt there was an animal in the room with me. You know, like a jackal—or a hyena. It was like seeing him for the first time, as he really was. Then he said something strange.

What did he say?

She leaned forwards, over the table, her cigarette held in the air off to one side. I'm in the concrete business, he said. Did I tell you that? I don't know, I said. Maybe. I probably wasn't listening.

I was grinning again. Why bring up the concrete business?

You know those stories you always hear about people being buried in the foundations of buildings and bridges?

I nodded.

He told me they were all true. Most bodies, he said, they're never found. Girls like you, they disappear. They're never seen again.

I stared at her. Was he threatening to kill you?

He wouldn't dare. He's weak. She paused. Also, he's a friend of my father's.

Wait a minute, I said. You went out with a friend of your father's?

She gave a little shrug, then extinguished her cigarette.

Shocking though it was, I had enjoyed hearing about the affair. I wasn't entirely sure why she had told me. I hadn't talked about the girls I'd slept with, not that there was much to say. Back then, I was often wasted, and I had made some bad choices. But Franca had come out of it well, with credit, and perhaps that was reason enough. I was amazed at how she'd stood up for herself. To look at her, you wouldn't have expected it. You'd have thought she'd be timid—maybe even beg, the way the concrete man had hoped she would. There was a shamelessness about her—an audacity— that I couldn't help admiring. *This is what I've done. Deal with it.*

Giacomo walked over and asked if she wanted coffee. Before she decided, he said, she should be aware that it was the best coffee in Abruzzo. He sourced the beans from a special roastery in Naples. Giacomo was known for his extravagant claims, but at the same time I knew that people came to his place from all over, especially in the morning. Sit there for long enough, and you'd meet every kind of person—lawyers, politicians, road sweepers, nightclub owners, fishermen, police.

Along with the coffee, Giacomo brought glasses of his homemade mandarin liqueur. On the house, he said. Green as kryptonite, the drink clashed beautifully with his shirt and trousers.

I looked across at Franca. Do you remember when we found Harry sitting on the bench that overlooks the valley? He was wearing a big dark coat and a wide-brimmed hat, like someone in a Western. We told him that we thought what he did on Halloween was great. I didn't go too far? he said. And we said no—both at the same time. That made him smile.

Why are you talking about Harry?

There was a moment when he looked at us and asked if we were friends. I think we nodded. He told us that when you find people who make you feel good, you should hold on to them. We didn't do it, though. We didn't hold on to what we had.

Eyes lowered, Franca stubbed out the cigarette that she was smoking. Not through any fault of mine.

I know, I said. I was lost. I didn't know what I was doing.

I thought of you. I often wondered where you were.

Did you? A shaft of regret went through me. Some-times people know more about us than we know our-selves, but we don't hear them when they speak. We're too busy with our own thoughts, which are near-sighted, muddled. Loud.

It's all right, she said. You're here now.

Something gave in me just then, like scaffolding no longer needed. She didn't have any intention of hold-ing me responsible for anything or blaming me. What she cared about was what was happening tonight, and what might happen next. Perhaps the story she had told me was her way of saying that I wasn't the only one who had strayed. She had behaved badly too. We were, in some sense, equal or the same.

Stepping on to the terrace, Giacomo lit a cigarette and stood facing out into the piazza.

So, kids, he said, enjoy the meal?

Everything was so fresh, Franca said. I could really taste the sea. She paused. Except for in the coffee.

Giacomo chuckled, then glanced across at me. I like this one. She's got spirit.

I had always known that she was special, but on that warm night in San Salvo Marina, in a restaurant be-longing to a man who had three testicles, something seemed to have been confirmed. She was special—but not just that. If I wanted, I could ask her out, and we could be together. I knew she was open to that. She wouldn't have agreed to see me otherwise. She wasn't about to make the first move, though. She had tried that once before, on the road to the convent. This time it would be up to me. Even so, I didn't feel that I should rush things. When I drove her back to the apartment that she shared with two other girls, I didn't try to kiss her or ask if I could come in. Instead, I thanked her for having dinner with me, and then I said good night and drove away. I thought I saw her in my rearview mirror, watching me go, a puzzled fondness on her face, as if I had wrong-footed her, but in a way she found intriguing or endearing—though if the truth be told I couldn't really have seen all that, could I? It was dark, and I only glanced in the mirror for a second. Perhaps that was the effect I hoped I'd had. Certainly, I didn't want to be predictable, like that concrete man she'd gone out with, but at the same time I couldn't be so unpredictable that I lost the opportunity that I was being offered. Because that was how I saw it suddenly, as an opportunity, a chance to turn my life around and make something decent of myself.

San Salvo is a nightmare to get out of. You think you've left the town behind, and all at once, mysteriously, you're right back in the center. Or else you find yourself trapped in the *zona industriale*—a sprawling maze of roundabouts, warehouses, pylons, fenced-off factories, parked trucks, and potholes. Someone in the *comune* should really sort it out. My strategy has always been to follow the signs to Isernia and then turn off at Fondovalle Treste. The Isernia road is straight and fast, with only one lane in each direction, and everybody drives like they're being pursued by demons, but you can reach my village in twenty minutes. That night, luckily, the road was empty—it was late—and when I saw a lorry parked in the lay-by up ahead, hazard lights flashing, I thought nothing of it. The next thing I knew, there was a loud crack, and a tiger flew past my windscreen, its mouth open in a snarl. Before I had time to make sense of what I had seen, three or four more tigers appeared, scattered across the road in front of me. I stamped on the brake, then swerved, fetching up against the crash barrier.

When I got out of the car, a man was standing there, a silhouette against the lorry's fierce headlights. He asked me if I had hit one of the tigers. I said I had. I wasn't hurt, though. We need to get them off the road, he said, before somebody gets killed. I followed him through the gap between the side of the truck and the crash barrier. I could smell scorched rubber, human sweat. He must have braked hard the moment he realized what was happening. Several tigers were lying on the road. They had outstretched paws and brightly colored saddles. Part of a merry-go-round, I thought. As always, there had been a funfair in San Salvo that summer, but the season had finished and the attractions were being dismantled.

One by one, we picked up the tigers and carried them to the lay-by. Though life-size, they were made of aluminum or fiberglass and didn't weigh too much. It was the work of a few moments. Still, I kept glancing nervously in both directions. If something came, it would come at speed. The Isernia road was one of the few cross-country routes that linked the Adriatic with cities like Rome and Naples, and it was never quiet for very long.

When we had recovered the last tiger, I peered into the back of the truck. It wasn't just tigers that were stacked up in the dark. Further in, there were prancing horses with plumes on their heads. There was even a giraffe.

Suddenly, a petrol tanker went past in a blast of hot wind, horn blaring.

I don't know how it happened, the lorry driver said. The tailgate must have come loose. He turned to me quickly, guiltily. I didn't ask about your car.

Headlights showed behind him, in the distance.

Listen, I said. I drank a lot this evening. I'd rather not be here if the carabinieri turn up.

The man put a hand on my shoulder. You've helped enough, son. You get yourself home.

I got back into my father's car and drove on.

It was only five minutes later, when I took the Fondovalle Treste turning, that I realized I was trembling. I kept imagining a tiger leaping towards the windscreen, claws outstretched, teeth bared. Though I was on a country road, I slowed right down. From time to time, I glanced through my side window at the dark hills and the trees in their neat rows beneath, the olives still a few weeks short of being picked.

The next day, when I told my father what had happened, he seemed to react in slow motion.

A tiger? he said, passing a hand up over his forehead and into his sparse hair. There aren't any tigers in Abruzzo.

Why was he being so obtuse? Sometimes I thought he did it deliberately.

Not a real one, I said. It was from a fairground. It fell off the back of a lorry.

A tiger, he said again.

He was having trouble imagining it. Also, he probably thought that I was lying. I had crashed his car, and now I was inventing a tall tale as an excuse.

If you don't believe me, I said, come and see.

Once outside, I made him bend down and inspect the orange streaks on the bumper and the coachwork. He seemed to think that I had faked that too. Even if there had been a clump of striped and bloody fur stuck to the headlight, he wouldn't have believed me. Even if there had been a sabertooth embedded in the radiator grille. He should never have allowed me to borrow his car. I was reckless, irresponsible. I always would be. That was what he was thinking.

When I told him that he wasn't to worry, and that I would have the car repaired, and that it would soon be as good as new, he muttered something to himself, then he set off down the hill, towards his allotment, one hand showing in the air above his shoulder, as if to say, Don't make promises that you can't keep.

I saw Franca, I shouted after him, like you wanted me to.

He didn't stop, or even look around.

I took her out to dinner, I shouted.

He just kept going.

I was so angry that I could have murdered him right there and then, and burned down all his precious tomato plants.


Franca spent the following weekend at her parents' apartment near the sports ground. When I called for her on Saturday evening, it was her mother, Silvana, who answered the door. She looked at me carefully, one hand on the doorframe, the other on her hip, her eyes guarded, almost black. Silvana worked in a pharmacy in

Gissi, but she had an occult air about her, I had always thought, like a clairvoyant or a witch.

How are you, Gino? she said. I haven't seen you in ages.

I'm fine, thank you, I said. Everything's much better now I'm back in touch with Franca. I looked down at my feet, then up at Silvana again. She's good for me.

Silvana gave me a smile that felt a little like a warning. I hope that goes both ways.

I hope so too, I said.

I hadn't seen Franca since our dinner in San Salvo, and later, as we sat on a bench that overlooked the valley, I told her about the weird incident on the Isernia road, after I dropped her off.

Weren't you in your father's car that night? Head bent, she was rolling a cigarette.

I told him I'll pay for it. He's still not happy.

She lit her roll-up and blew smoke at the view.

When someone's waiting for you to make a mess of things, I went on, it's almost impossible not to.

The rooks whirled away from the church, as they often did, squabbling and cackling, and dark as fragments of charred paper lifting off a fire. Down in the valley everything was quiet, the vineyards and olive trees made vague and furtive by the slowly gathering blue dusk.

Franca was nodding. All those tigers, though. You could see it as good fortune—a kind of gift.

Good fortune? I wasn't sure I understood.

Exotic animals appearing unexpectedly, she said, just as you happen to pass by. Like you were on safari. People pay a lot for that.

I laughed out loud.

She flicked her dead roll-up through a gap in the railings. Buy me a drink?

The bar in the main piazza was crowded, but luckily none of the boys I had grown up with were there. I had dreaded the comments they would be bound to make when they saw me out with Franca. Sitting by the wall, drinking a beer, was my mother's cousin, Pasquale. He was known to have been wild in his youth. He'd had lots of girlfriends, but he had never married. These days, he made wine in his *cantina* and smoked a bit of weed, and that was about it. With his wavy, graying hair and his acne scars, he still had a kind of glamour, though. Perhaps because my father disapproved of Pasquale, I had always been drawn to him. He nodded as we entered. We stopped to say hello, but didn't join him.

After finishing our drinks, we walked to the east end of the village and sat side by side, halfway down a steep flight of steps. A streetlamp attached to the wall of a nearby house gave off an eerie light. Below us, like a mosaic, were all the rooftops, the curved tiles laid out in rows, and crusted with lichen. Beyond them, the land rose to a wooded ridge. The valley lay in between, invisible. From somewhere, faintly, came the call of a tawny owl, urgent and haunting.

I looked sidelong at Franca. Do you remember what you said to me when you were nine?

In the alley's dim green glow, her eyes were as black as her mother's.

Of course I remember. Her voice had softened, as if I had taken her back in time. As if she was in the playground, and I was sitting in the corner, reading a comic.

I admired you for it.

Really?

I thought it took real nerve. I knew what it would cost you—you know, in terms of being teased.

Oh, I was teased all right.

Why me, though? I mentioned the popular boys at school, the boys who girls glanced at surreptitiously, or whispered about behind their hands. Why not one of them?

I wouldn't have stood a chance with them, she said. With you, it was different.

I tried to smile, but couldn't help feeling wounded.

She nudged my shoulder. You're taking this the wrong way.

How should I take it, then?

You and me, she said. We had more power than they did.

I looked at her, waiting for an explanation.

They had all the advantages, she went on, and we had none. We had to fight for everything. We had to be stronger than they were.

More power, I said. I never thought of it like that.

Just then, I had the sense that things were shifting or being rearranged. The future had moved closer.

And what do you think now? I went on. Do you feel the same?

Nothing's changed, she said.

I turned to her, and she turned a moment later. It was a clumsy kiss—I missed half her mouth—but then I adjusted, or she did, and the kiss deepened. My heart began to glide. One of her hands was at the back of my neck, in my hair. The color behind my eyelids was a warm brown glow, like melted sugar.

I'm yours, Gino, she murmured. I always have been.

There had been times in my life when I thought that what was being withheld was more attractive than what was already on offer. Only the unattainable was worth pursuing. That night, on the alley steps, it seemed the opposite was true.

It's such a warm night, I said. Why don't we go up to Colle San Giovanni?

I was walking Franca back to her parents' apartment. It was after midnight, and the bar had closed.

How would we get there? she asked.

I don't know. My father's car?

I thought you crashed it.

I hit a tiger, that's all. The car still works.

She grinned.

When we reached my house, the lights were off. I was aware of my parents inside, in the dark. Telling Franca to wait for me on the drive, I entered the house by the side door. I moved on tiptoe, trying not to make a sound. The car keys were where they always were, on a hook on the kitchen wall. I also took a bottle of plum brandy from the sideboard.

Outside again, I stopped in the shadow of the pomegranate tree. Franca was leaning against my father's car, her face tilted upwards, as if to gather light from the stars or the moon. In that moment, I felt lucky. Who wrote that luck and death go hand in hand? I don't believe it. My luck had to do with how she saw me. Who she was. She hadn't held my long absence against me. She had known that I would come for her eventually. And when I appeared, she was ready, not burdened in the slightest by impatience or resentment.

Franca, I said.

She smiled at me across one shoulder. I moved out from beneath the tree, then took her in my arms and kissed her. I loved the feel of her chipped tooth against my tongue. That tiny missing piece.

You taste of strawberries, I said.

I do?

No one ever told you that?

She shook her head.

When I was six or seven, I said, my parents took me to Nemi, for the strawberry festival. That's what you remind me of. I paused. Do you know the story?

What story?

According to legend, Adonis was killed not far from Nemi. When Venus heard that he was dead, she couldn't stop crying. She had told him not to go hunting, but he was too full of himself, and he hadn't listened. As she held him, her tears mingled with his blood, and when they dropped to the earth they turned into strawberries.

That's beautiful, Franca said. Kiss me again.

I couldn't afford to wake my father, so I used a technique I had used before. After releasing the handbrake, I pushed the car backwards, onto the road, then we climbed in and freewheeled down the hill. Only when we were out of earshot did I start the engine.

I don't want you to get into trouble. Franca was sitting low in the seat, with her feet propped on the dashboard and her knees pulled up against her chest.

He gets up at five, I told her. We'll be back before then.

Five? But it's Sunday tomorrow.

The moon's almost full. It's his last chance to do any planting. I looked across at her. You always plant when the moon's waxing. That's one of his rules.

My father believes that too, she said. If you want to pick grapes or olives, or take things from the ground, you wait until the moon's on the wane. She paused. Also if you want to kill a pig.

By the time we reached Liscia, which was on the far side of the valley, and nearly twice as high as Caracciolo, it was after one o'clock. I drove through the deserted piazza, then up the hill towards the pine forest. Five minutes later, I was parking on a flat, unpaved area next to the road. I took charge of the plum brandy, and Franca tucked a blanket from the boot under one arm. We had fallen quiet. As we climbed the gentle slope, there was only the rustle of our footsteps and the smell of dry grass. In the moonlight, the patches of pale rock looked phosphorescent.

We came out on the top of the hill. During the day, the mountains of Gran Sasso and the Maiella would be visible to the north. Off to the east were the towns of Casalbordino and Vasto, two clusters of lights, with the blackness of the Adriatic Sea beyond. To the south, the view extended into Molise, even into Puglia.

You can see everything from here, I said.

Franca let the blanket drop. It was as if she had taken off something that she was wearing, and I thought of that night in the convent, years ago. The flame of the candle, the straight line of the smoke. The look on her face, heated and unflinching. She murmured a few words that I didn't catch, then she was reaching up, and her mouth was on my mouth, and one of her hands was flat against my chest, where my heart was.

Spreading the blanket on the ground, we lay down and rid ourselves of all our clothes. The warm air moved across my skin. When I entered her, I seemed to leave myself behind. Later, I heard her cry out, but it came from a distance, then I was on my back with her head against my shoulder, her thin arm flung across my ribs.

Don't say anything, she said.

I stared upwards into the blackness, which was pulsing, limitless. I thought of deep space, and us at the edge of it, but also part of it, as if we had been offered up, and I felt safe, even though I was naked. Somehow, the size and nearness of the sky protected me.

Gino?

Once again, her voice seemed to come from far away, though she couldn't have been closer.

I think I fell asleep, I said.

We should go, she said. It's getting late.

I sat up and looked around. As yet, no light showed in the east, where the sea was. The darkness seemed unsettled, though. I reached for the plum brandy, pulled out the cork, and handed it to her. She drank from the bottle and handed it back. I did the same, then corked the bottle and held her again, the warmth of the alcohol pooling inside me, her cool body against mine, her long hair. Our village lay below us, across the valley.

It's like a crocodile, don't you think? I said.

Franca turned in my arms.

I reached out a hand, pointing. That's the crocodile's body, where most of the houses are. But look at the two roads that lead west. They're the jaws. See how they're gaping open?

She shivered a little. I never thought of it like that.

It wasn't me who thought of it, I said. Pasquale told me, when he brought me up here once.

I don't remember what we talked about as we drove back. Perhaps we didn't talk at all. Perhaps there was no need. If we were silent, though, it was an easy silence, just as it had been when we were young. I remember her tilting the bottle to her lips, then passing it to me, her eyes on the uneven, twisting road ahead, and it thrilled me that she knew exactly where I was. She didn't have to look. I remember my heart expanding, it seemed twice its normal size, but the feeling wasn't squeamish, it was more like a rush or a glow, and I remember stopping at the junction where the red house was and kissing her, the taste of plums with strawberries beneath.

If my father ever suspected me of taking his car, he didn't mention it. On Monday evening I was able to collect my Lancia from the mechanic. At the end of that week, I met Franca after work, and we drove north, up the Adriatica. The old main road follows the coastline. There are tall palm trees, and sharp sprays of aloe vera, and hidden, rocky coves. There are seaside villas topped with balustrades and urns. Always scornful of seat belts, Franca was leaning against the door, with one leg tucked beneath her. The windows were open, and her long hair blew across her face. I worried about her falling out, but I didn't say anything. If she wanted to think of herself as reckless and carefree, who was I to intervene?

When I reached Casarza, I pulled off the road and parked in a small car park that gave access to the beach. The sky above the horizon looked sullen, dark gray with a suggestion of mauve. Beneath it, the sea was an eerie, milky-pale green. No waves broke against the shore. Instead, there was a stirring in the water, a kind of stifled restlessness.

I led Franca down a track until we reached a padlocked gate. It was so warm and humid that the air seemed to part as you moved through it. On the other side of the gate, half-hidden in the undergrowth, was a weather-stained white caravan.

What is this place? she asked.

It belongs to somebody called Razor, I told her. It was one of our hangouts in the bad old days.

How do you know he isn't here?

It's unlikely. Last I heard, he was in Torre Sinello.

The prison?

He robbed a petrol station.

I called his name, then waited. Nothing happened. I called again.

As I thought, I said. There's nobody around.

I climbed over the gate, then helped Franca to climb over. The door to the caravan was locked, and the curtains were drawn. We moved on down the slope, between tall stands of cane. There were charred patches on the ground where fires had been built. Faded plastic chairs stood up against a hedge. I went off into the long grass and picked a couple of red-orange fruit from a small tree and gave one to Franca. She took a bite.

It doesn't taste of much, she said.

I know, I said. Good color, though.

I flung mine into the bushes.

At the far end of the plot of land, before the big brown rocks and the steep drop to the beach, there was a cane pergola and a table made from two cheap trestles and an old front door. Bleached skulls and rusty hurricane lamps were mounted on poles, and someone had strung fishing floats on a dangling length of twine, like an upright necklace or a kebab. There was a one-room tree house that could be reached by climbing a ladder. The door was just a gap, and there was no wall on the side that faced the sea, only a wooden railing. I had slept there once, when I was nineteen or twenty. I'd never had such vivid dreams.

I dumped my rucksack on the table and unpacked. I had brought bread and cheese, some prosciutto, and a bottle of Pasquale's Montepulciano. I foraged in the bottom of the bag, then let out an exasperated sigh.

I forgot the candles, I said.

Franca put a hand on my shoulder. You don't have to try so hard.

Later, when it was almost dark, she told me that she wanted us to live together. We were lying, half-naked, in the tree house. Off to the right, beyond the rocks, was a *trabocco*, the wooden jetty stretching out over the sea on stilts. At the end was a hut that would once have been a fish restaurant. The structure looked black and spiky, like an ancient crustacean, and the water rose and fell beneath it, like something breathing.

I want to go to sleep with you, she said. Wake up with you.

Where would we live?

She leaned up on one elbow and looked at me, her expression earnest and intent. I don't know. But you'd be happy to?

Before I could answer, I heard men's voices, then a rattle of metal. Somebody was trying the gate. I scrambled over to the doorway. As I peered towards the top of the garden, the gate burst open. Three shadowy figures stood in the half-light. One of them lit a cigarette, and the flash of the lighter's flame showed me a tattooed wrist and a gold tooth.

Get dressed, I said to Franca. Quick.

We threw on our clothes, then climbed down the ladder and crouched in the shadows at the foot of the tree. The men were ambling down the slope, fanned out in a loose line, as if to stop us escaping.

Anybody here? one called out.

They had a swagger, as if they owned the place, or didn't care who owned it, and their laughter was harsh, like gulls. I didn't think they'd seen us yet. They would have noticed the car, though.

I nudged Franca.

Follow me, I whispered. And stay low.

We climbed down over the big, brown rocks, then hurried along the beach. I could taste blood, as if I had been running. Would they hear our footsteps on the stones? I didn't dare look round. We crept up the steps that led to the car park, still keeping low. Three motorbikes stood near my car. One had a skull painted on the petrol tank. By now, the men would have found the remains of our picnic. They would know that someone had been there recently. We ran to my car and got in. Starting the engine, I sped out of the car park, up the curving slope and back onto the Adriatica. Would they come after us? I kept glancing in the rearview mirror, but saw no motorbikes.

Who were they? Franca's voice was small, unsure. She sounded shaken, unlike herself.

I don't know, I said. I never saw them before.

Were they Razor's friends?

I don't know.

Something bad would have happened, wouldn't it, she said, if they had caught us.

That's what it felt like.

She was quiet for a few moments. Lucky you forgot the candles, she said after a while.

When I stopped at a red light, I glanced in the rearview mirror again. Still no bikes.

I think we're okay, I said.

I drove through Vasto, then on towards San Salvo. I had agreed to stay at Franca's apartment that night.

That man you used to go out with, I said. How would I find him?

Which man?

The one with the concrete business.

She turned to look at me. Why would you want to find him?

I'd like to speak to him.

That's not a good idea.

What if I need to, for my peace of mind?

He's not worth the trouble. Really. She shifted in her seat. What would you say to him, anyway?

I don't know. I'd just like to speak to him.

Forget it, she said.

A few nights later, I dropped in on Pasquale. Sitting with him in the kitchen were Harry French and a burly man with a moustache. Dinner was finished, and the three men had pushed their chairs back from the table. Pasquale's dog, Nada, had put her nose on his thigh, and he was stroking her absentmindedly. As always, the Roman radio station, Radio Capital, was on in the next room, playing music from the seventies and eighties.

Pasquale fetched me a glass, then introduced me to the man with the moustache.

This is Dante, he said. He has a restaurant in Cupello. We should all go and eat there soon.

Once, when I was much younger, I had driven through Cupello with Pasquale, and he had told me a curious fact about the village. Its inhabitants were famous for having big heads. He didn't mean that they were arrogant or proud. He was referring to an actual physical phenomenon. As he spoke, a woman stepped out of a butcher's. There, Pasquale cried triumphantly. You see? There was no denying it. The woman's head was enormous. As we left the village, though, we passed a man with a perfectly normal head. If anything, in fact, it was on the small side. What about him? I said. That guy? Pasquale said. He's from some-where else.

I shook hands with Dante, then sat down next to Harry. I hadn't seen him for several months, not since the late spring. I asked when he'd got back.

Two days ago, he said.

Look at you, I said. You're pale as a ghost.

Harry gave me his usual tight-lipped smile. I was in Wales for the summer, with the wife.

Was it cold?

Freezing, he said. What about you, Gino? What have you been up to?

He's seeing Marcello's daughter, Pasquale said. Mar-cello the ambulance driver.

Harry looked at him. You mean Franca?

Pasquale nodded.

How did you know? I asked him.

The other night, he said. In the bar. He relit his roll-up. I'm not fucking blind.

After that, I didn't get a moment's peace. *Marcello's not going to be happy, is he, his daughter going with the likes of you. Of all the sons-in-law to be saddled with. I wouldn't be surprised if he loses it completely and puts you in the hospital. He'll probably drive you there himself.* The jokes kept com-ing. Even Dante, who I had never met before, joined in with the teasing. But I was proud to be with Franca, and I didn't care who knew. Also, if Marcello was going to put anybody in the hospital, it would surely be his friend, the concrete man. Though I couldn't say that, of course. Franca had sworn me to secrecy.

Next thing we know, Dante said, she'll be dragging him to the altar.

I reached for my wine and drank. She wouldn't have to drag me, I said. I'd go quite willingly.

The three men chuckled to themselves. They were older than me, and they knew better.

So your father's car's fixed, then? Pasquale said.

I nodded. Good as new.

Pasquale turned to Harry. Gino hit a tiger the other day.

Interesting, Harry said. I hit a deer once, in Scotland. I've never hit a tiger, though.

The three men began swapping stories of incidents involving cars and wild animals. Later, Dante sang a traditional Abruzzese song, and Pasquale kept time by tapping objects on the table with a fork. Dante's voice was so loud that the walls vibrated. In his enthusiasm, Pasquale knocked a hole in the side of a glass. Harry looked on, his tight-lipped smile unwavering.

Later still, when Harry and Dante had gone, I asked Pasquale if he knew of a man with a concrete business. Apparently, he was a friend of Franca's father.

That would be Pierozzi, he said. Enzo Pierozzi. What about him?

I was just wondering where his business is.

It's just off the Adriatica, not far from Ortona. Pasquale looked at me, his dark eyes calm but curious, shadow seeming to deepen the pockmarks on his face. Why do you want to know?

I told him a story about a work colleague who was thinking of having a swimming pool built, then I glanced at my watch. It was almost one in the morning.

I thanked Pasquale for the drink and left.


Towards the end of that month I took half a day off work, claiming that I had a dental appointment. As I drove north, making for Ortona, I remembered the exchange I'd had with my boss, Raul, and I couldn't help but smile. Raul had looked surprised when I informed him of the appointment. I thought you saw the dentist a couple of weeks ago, he said. That was the doctor, I told him. What's wrong with you, Gino? he said. Are you some kind of hypochondriac? On the contrary, I said. Regular medical checkups are the key to good health. Raul stared at me, nonplussed. Maybe that's something you should think about, chief, I said, now you're in your fifties. Raul was shaking his head, like the old sheep that he was. Get along with you, he said, you cheeky so-and-so.

My smile faded as the concrete plant appeared. I drove in through the gates and parked next to a black

Range Rover. The one-story prefab office backed onto a row of trees, their sparse foliage almost white with dust. Inside the office, behind a desk, was a middle-aged woman in a zebra-print blouse. Her dyed blonde hair stirred stiffly in the breeze from the fan in the corner. She was talking on the phone, but she looked at me and nodded, acknowledging my presence.

When the call had finished, I asked if I could see Mr. Pierozzi. She pointed through the window at a man in a white shirt and a white hard hat who was crossing the tarmac. That's him.

I caught up with Pierozzi in the shadow of a massive silver silo.

Excuse me, I said.

He stopped and turned. How can I help?

His voice was soft, like the sort of voice I imagined a hypnotist might have—though I had never actually been to see a hypnotist. This was the voice that had said, Girls like you, they disappear. Now I thought about it, I found it strange that Franca hadn't felt more threatened—that she hadn't been scared, in fact—but perhaps, in telling the story, she had pretended to be tougher than she was, or perhaps she had been drawing on the same nerve that she had showed in the school playground when she was nine.

But if I hadn't spoken yet, it was nothing to do with Pierozzi's voice. It was because I had been utterly wrong-footed by his appearance. Franca had described him as "weak," and I suppose, as a result, I had been expecting someone who was relatively ordinary or nondescript—a receding hairline, narrow shoulders, a potbelly—but Pierozzi was almost shockingly good-looking. He had dark eyes and white teeth, and his short-sleeved shirt revealed strong forearms that were covered in black hair. As I considered him, I noticed that his face had hardened. Clearly, I wasn't your typical customer or client. I had studied him too carefully. I had taken too long.

You had an affair with Franca, I said.

Pierozzi held my gaze, small muscles flexing in his well-shaped jaw. Who?

Franca Magliani. You had an affair with her.

I don't know what you're on about.

He was someone who was accustomed to being in command of any given situation. Though caught off guard, he wasn't about to give that up.

When she ended it, I said, you threatened her—

He laughed in my face. Who the fuck are you?

If you threaten her again, I said, or go anywhere near her, your wife will find out, and so will her father, and your whole world will fall apart. All this— and I gestured at the storage silos, the transfer belts, and the loading hoppers—all this will be gone.

My wife doesn't have a father, you clown. He died ten years ago.

*You clown.*

I smiled. Just stay away from her. Don't try to contact her. Don't even—

He moved up close and put a finger against my chest. It felt solid and brutal, like a cattle prod. You think you can come in here and tell me what to do? he said in his soft voice. Stepping back, he jerked his head towards the main gate. Get lost.

As I drove home, I was convinced that I had had an effect on him, even though he had admitted nothing and had called me names. He would think about what I had said. In retrospect, I was no longer entirely sure why I had engineered the confrontation. It wasn't because I wanted to intimidate the man or warn him off. It seemed unlikely that he would have troubled Franca again. His threats against her had been empty posturing, a consequence of wounded pride, nothing more sinister than that. In fact, he was probably relieved that the affair was over, and that he'd got away with it. Who knows, he might even have started seeing someone else. He seemed the type. No, I thought, as I pulled into the Portobello service station, the reason I had done what I had done was a selfish one. If I was to be with Franca, I needed to clear the ground. I didn't want the past to interfere with the present. It had to be erased or buried, as though it had never been.

That Friday, after work, I met Franca at the Vanity Café on the outskirts of San Salvo. As we sat on the terrace with our drinks, she told me that she had been to see Agnese, a distant cousin of her father's. Agnese lived in an apartment in Casalbordino, but she also owned a house in the country. She knew she ought to sell the place—she should probably have sold it years ago—but she could never quite bring herself to part with it, even though it was standing empty. It was where she had spent her childhood. All her memories were there. At the same time, she knew she would never live in the house again, not with her bad legs and her failing eyesight.

Franca reached for her glass. When I asked if I could move in with my boyfriend, she liked the idea. She saw it as a way of keeping the house in the family. She finished her beer. It's a bit off the beaten track, but it would be cheap. Would you come and look at it tomorrow?

Smiling, I sat back. You don't waste much time, do you.

The next day, when I called at her parents' apartment to pick her up, it was her father who answered the door. There were pouches under his eyes, and he hadn't shaved.

How are you, Mr. Magliani? I said.

I'm good. Keeping his eyes on me, he called over his shoulder. Franca?

Franca appeared next to him, in a black crop top and cutoff jeans. She gave him a kiss on the cheek and told him she'd be back in time for dinner.

See you, Magliani said to me as I turned away. Or maybe it's better if I don't. He hung in the doorway, grinning.

Don't take it personally, Franca said once we were in my car. He says that to everyone.

I told her that I thought I'd heard him use the phrase before, when I was younger, but I'd never understood what he meant by it.

It's because he's an ambulance driver, she explained. If he sees you, he'll be in his ambulance, which means you'll be really ill, or badly injured, or maybe even dead. So it's better if he doesn't see you. She sighed. He thinks it's hilarious.

It was at least half an hour's drive to Agnese's house, and Franca talked the whole way. In her mind, we were already living there. She had it all worked out. We would get up early, she was saying. She would make me a coffee, and then we would leave together. It would be best if we headed straight to the Isernia road. It was only fifteen minutes in the car, and we'd see nothing on the way, only a derelict farmhouse, or a tractor hauling a trailer heaped with grapes, or a man with a gun, out hunting. After that, it would take no time to get to San Salvo—so long as we didn't come across any tigers, that is. Rumor had it there were tigers in the area. Though I smiled, I couldn't help thinking that she was going too fast. How could she have so much faith in us, and in our future as a couple?

We circled Palmoli, then dropped down into the valley. When we reached a fork in the road, she told me to bear left. A small house stood on the corner. Washing hung on a line at the back. Blue work trousers. Underpants. A man living on his own.

Our house is further on, Franca said. Our house is bigger.

*Our house.*

We hadn't even seen it yet.

I slowed down. The tarmac had split open lengthways, and grass and weeds grew in the cracks. Through the bushes and the evergreens, I sometimes glimpsed the mountains to the south. Franca was leaning forwards, one hand on the dashboard. We passed another house. There was no glass in the windows, but the roof was good, its tiles weighed down at the edges by large rocks.

It's not that one either, she said.

Power lines ran parallel to the road. Despite the middle-of-nowhere feeling, this wasn't land that had been neglected or left to rot.

There. She was pointing through the windscreen.

Beyond a fir tree was a long low house with a gray facade. But it was the cloud that I noticed first. The only cloud in an otherwise clear sky, it curved above the tiled roof, soft and white and elongated, like a feather boa dropped by an heiress or a model on her way out of a party. There it lay, accidental yet significant, like the symbol of a life that I could only dream of. Or perhaps—just perhaps—this was the life I was dreaming of, right here.

Franca, I called out. Did you see the cloud?

She had walked ahead of me, into the long grass, but she turned at the sound of my voice. I caught up with her and held her in my arms.

I was right about this place, she said, looking away from me, across the land.

I didn't believe you.

You do now, though, don't you.

Taking my hand, she led me round to the front. Along with the borage that grew wild on the rough ground, I also recognized mustard and fennel and milk thistle. Some of my father's knowledge had lodged in me, despite all my attempts to resist it. Beyond the fig trees that marked the edge of the property, the land dropped away. The steep, wooded gulley opened out into a scoop-shaped valley that was soaked in sunlight, the distant fields and meadows a radiant, exaggerated yellow-green. Mountains rose beyond, their slopes sprinkled here and there with the white and gray of villages. Though I was standing close to the house, there was a spaciousness to the air, a sensation you might have if you entered a room with a particularly high ceiling.

With it came the conviction that I had somehow stepped out of time. I turned to Franca, wanting to try and convey what I was feeling, but she spoke first.

I think I've been here before.

In another life? I said.

No, in this one. When I was a child.

She described a sunlit afternoon with people eating at a table in the shadow of the trees. A woman wore a white dress. A man stood up and sang.

It sounds like a wedding, I said.

She held up a key. Shall we go in?

Agnese had told her that an artist had lived in the house in the nineties, but only during the summer months, when it was warm. Since then, people must have broken in, as the walls were covered with graffiti. GO SSC NAPOLI. SMASH FASCISM. NO TAV. FUCK THE STATE. MARIO LOVES FRANCESCA. On the ground floor there were two rooms—a kitchen with a fireplace, and a room with a round table and four chairs. Stairs led up to a landing or corridor that ran the entire length of the house, with three bedrooms off it, and a bathroom at the end. Here, too, we found evidence of intruders—a dirty sleeping bag, some empty bottles, a pile of comic books, a crushed cigarette packet, a used condom.

Returning from the bathroom, I called Franca's name.

In here, she called back.

I found her in the middle bedroom. She had opened the shutters, and she was leaning on the sill, her right foot balanced on the back of her left ankle. Her hair fell past her shoulders, almost to the leather belt she was wearing to hold up her shorts. I went and stood beside her at the window. Now we were on the first floor, the fig trees no longer hid the view. It was late afternoon. The sun had dropped in the sky, and the light had the dull gold quality of old gilt picture frames. Apart from two villages on far-off ridges, there was no evidence of human beings, no sign of any kind of life.

This reminds me of being in the convent, I said, when we were young—that feeling of being alone together, in our own secret world.

She turned to me. There's one big difference, isn't there. We don't have to leave. I could feel her breath on my face. We were that close. Maybe we could live here forever, she said. Like people in a fairy tale.


The following weekend, we went to visit Franca's aunt Agnese in her apartment in Casalbordino. She lived near the main piazza, in a palazzo with a crumbling shield above the entrance. She almost never left the building, Franca told me. She had difficulty walking.

As Franca poured three glasses of Saronno, Agnese spoke to us from her chair by the window. The one great advantage of her apartment was the view, she told us, the way the land sloped away below her, down to the Adriatic. Sometimes the strip of sea was so blue that it didn't look real. She couldn't remember the last time she went for a swim. Swimming seemed like something impossible and fantastic now. She reached for her glass with a trembling hand, then brought it to her lips and drank. She had a round face with thin, arched eyebrows, and her gray hair was chopped off just beneath her ears.

We saw the house, Franca said. We loved it.

It was called La Peschiera, Agnese told us. There used to be a large fishpond that was stocked with perch and tench and rainbow trout. In the past, there were many fishponds in the area. They sold to local people, and also to restaurants. Most, if not all, had been filled in. Her father had lived in the house, she went on, and his father before him. They worked on the land. Grew things. Her gaze drifted to the window. They led simple lives, she said. They went unnoticed.

I remember a man singing, Franca said.

Agnese nodded. You were there when you were little—for Sunday lunches, family celebrations.

Good things happened there, Franca said.

I wouldn't say that. There was a new edge to Agnese's voice. Ordinary things, she said. Some good, some not so good.

The place had a lovely feel to it, I said. A kind of timelessness. A sense of space. I thought for a moment. The sky felt taller than it usually does.

I don't know what that means. Agnese sipped her Saronno, then put the glass down carefully and turned to me. Franca's father was here the other day. He said you've had some problems in the past.

A memory came to me—the long, hot drive to the religious community in Liguria, and then my passport and my wallet being taken off me by a priest. *You're kidding, right?*

That was a long time ago, Franca said. He's over all that now.

Agnese was still observing me. And are you? she said. Over all that?

I took a breath, hauling myself back into the present.

I met Franca at the village school when I was nine, I told her, but then we lost touch and the years went by and I fell in with the wrong people. I did things that I'm not particularly proud of. I looked down at my hands. A clock was ticking somewhere close by. And then, a few weeks ago, I went on, I started thinking of her again. I had this strong feeling that I needed to see her, and that she would be the saving of me. And when I saw her again, in her office in San Salvo, I knew that it was true. I felt my life was changing, though I didn't know how exactly. It was just that if she was there in front of me, if she was with me, I could become a different person. A better person.

Agnese looked at Franca, then back at me. I wasn't expecting quite such a speech, she said. But her view of me seemed to have altered. She was warmer, and less appraising. Perhaps I had gone some way towards setting her mind at rest. All the same, I wondered what Franca's father had told her. I could see Marcello, with his shifty eyes, his swept-back hair. Which "problems" had he mentioned? I didn't like the thought that stories about me were still being passed around.

Half an hour later, it was settled. We could move into La Peschiera whenever we wanted, provided that we agreed to carry out the necessary renovations and take care of all the bills.

We clattered down the stone stairs and out onto the street, then we stood on the narrow pavement, facing in different directions, as if uncertain what to do next, and I wondered if Franca was thinking what I was thinking—that it was hard to believe that our lives, now we were together, were blessed with such good fortune. Surprising myself, I dropped to my knees in front of her.

Will you marry me, Franca?

She looked past me, along the street. The wind moved her hair, revealing an ear.

You shouldn't joke about such things.

I didn't know this was going to happen, I told her. I haven't got a ring or anything. I'm not joking, though. Will you marry me?

Returning my gaze, she understood that I was serious. She bent down and held my face in both her hands and kissed me.

A car sounded its horn as it went by.

Yes, she said. Yes, of course. Now she was kneeling too. It took you long enough.

I grinned. It's only been a month.

Or sixteen years, she said, depending on how you look at it.

We agreed to tell our parents about our plans, but it was several days before I found the right moment. After work on Thursday, I drove home under a low gray sky. In the mountains it was already raining. I sat at the kitchen table with a glass of wine while my mother sliced pigs' cheeks into thin strips. She was making spaghetti carbonara, my favorite pasta dish. I told her about my boss, Raul, and how unlucky he was. Once, he stepped into the road to avoid walking under a ladder and he tripped and fell into a drain. We shouldn't be laughing, my mother kept saying, but we couldn't stop, and then my father walked in, holding four pomegranates. He put the fruit on the table, then moved to the sink and washed his hands.

Did I miss something? he said.

My mother looked up from the chopping board. Gino was just telling me a funny story about his boss.

Nodding, my father opened the fridge, took out a bottle of beer, and poured a modest amount into a glass, but he showed no interest in what I had been saying. Instead, he began to talk about his olive trees, and how he thought that we would have to do the *raccolta* earlier this year.

I waited until dinner was almost over, then I said that I had an announcement to make. An apprehensive look rose onto my father's face. He would be wondering what kind of announcement it was. I doubted he'd be thinking it was good.

I asked Franca to marry me, I said, and she said yes.

Reaching across the table, my mother put a hand on my hand. That's wonderful, Gino.

You're getting married? My father had the fumbling look he often had.

Yes, I said.

For a moment or two, he didn't speak. If anything, his puzzlement appeared to intensify. Outside, the wind had got up. The shutters on the window rattled.

That seems a bit hasty, he said. A month ago, you didn't even know where she was living.

You told me that I needed to settle down, remember? I said. Well, I'm settling down.

Once again, he couldn't find any words. His hands moved on the table, one against the other, but slowly, very slowly, and I thought of the lobsters I had seen once in a fancy restaurant, in a glass tank.

You should be happy, I went on. If it hadn't been for you, it might never have happened.

He reached for one of the pomegranates, then took out the hunting knife that he carried everywhere with him and cut the fruit in half. A few bright drops of juice landed on the table.

These are just right, he said. I picked them this afternoon.

My mother's grip on my hand tightened. When would you like the wedding to take place?

As soon as possible, I said.

What's the hurry? she said. You need to be sure. And there are preparations to be made.

My father calmly and expertly dissected one half of the pomegranate, removing the white pith to reveal the jeweled red seeds.

I'm glad you've found someone, he said, his eyes still lowered.

You sound surprised, I said.

His eyes lifted. They seemed paler than usual, and oddly unengaged, as if he was impervious or immune to anything that I might say.

You didn't think anyone would have me, I said, did you.

That's not what he's saying, dear, my mother said.

All the same, I couldn't ignore the complete lack of interest that I saw in my father's eyes. To make matters worse, he had turned the whole situation on its head. He seemed to be trying to defend himself, as if I was the one who had been unenthusiastic or insulting, as if I was the aggressor. He had occupied ground that should rightfully have been mine. That *was* mine. Perhaps this was something he had always done.

Why can't you just be happy for me? I said.

I am happy for you, he said at last. If that's what you want. Of course I'm happy.

But he was behaving like someone in a hostage video. He was saying what he'd been forced to say. He didn't believe a word of it.

*If that's what you want.*

One other piece of news, I said. Obviously, I'll be moving out. I looked at my father across the table. At least that should make you happy.

He met my gaze for a few moments, then turned his attention back to the pomegranate that he was working on. I noticed that his hands had the same texture, tough and leathery. It was as if he had more in common with the pomegranate than he did with me. As if it was more of a son to him.

Fuck this, I said.

I threw down my napkin and rose to my feet, then I went round the table and bent over my mother and gave her a hug.

Thank you for dinner, I said.

She was crying, but trying not to show it.

Outdoors, it was like another version of the inside of my head. High winds and sideways rain. By the time I reached the steps that led down to the school, I was soaked. I had no idea where I was going. My only thought was to put some distance between myself and my father.

Five minutes later, I pushed through the door of the bar, wiping the rain from my face.

Give me a grappa, I said.

Well, well, a voice behind me said. Look who it is.

I swung round.

Luca was sitting on the corner with Giotto, a friend of his, the two of them hunched over the table like a couple of conspirators. Luca was wearing a brown leather jacket over a lilac shirt, and he had grown his hair. Knotted and tangled, it hung almost to his shoulders. I didn't know Giotto, though I had seen him around. He was always passing out when he overdid the drugs or drink. He'd got his nickname from an apartment building on Via Giotto in Foggia. It had collapsed one night, and most of the residents had died.

When the bar closed, Luca asked if I was coming

back with them. They were going to Giotto's great-aunt's place.

Only if you can sort me out, I said.

Luca made a quick noise with his tongue and teeth, letting me know that I was asking a question that didn't need asking.

An old man from the bar dropped us in the valley below the village. The woods closed over us. We turned off the road and onto a rough track. The rain had slackened. A modern two-story house loomed out of the darkness. The barking started, and there was a strong smell of shit. Dogs milled around us, pushing their muzzles into our hands.

Careful where you tread, Giotto said.

We stopped on the threshold of a bare, cave-like room. The TV was the only source of light. An ancient, shapeless woman in sunglasses was slumped in front of a variety show. She seemed fixated by the array of capped teeth, wigs, and silicone.

You boys want to watch TV?

Her voice was dry and papery, and she had a lump on her forehead, as if she had walked into something or fallen over.

Giotto told her we were going to his room.

Suit yourselves, she said.

The dogs aren't really hers, Giotto told us as we climbed the stairs. She takes in strays.

Not just dogs either, Luca said.

Giotto laughed.

Once in his room, he put on some drum and bass. Nervous, hypnotic beats. Round white pills on the palm of Luca's hand.

Take two, he said.

A white glow oozing from the fish tank, smoke in shifting layers near the ceiling.

Giotto wanted to know why I'd been sectioned. I was going to kill my father, I told him. I was out of my head. They had to call the carabinieri. I crushed my roll-up in the ashtray. I still want to kill him—sometimes.

Luca asked about rehab.

At the time it was a nightmare, I said, but now, weirdly, I have some good memories.

Like what?

Like getting up at four in the morning to make breakfast for the others, which meant I had the kitchen to myself. I'd drink a coffee and look out over the fields—rice fields going on forever, all the way to the horizon. The peacefulness of that. I paused. Smoking wasn't allowed, but we used to tear strips off the outside of cardboard boxes and roll them into tubes and smoke them. I paused again. They weren't bad, actually.

Luca shook his head, uncomprehending.

A lamp with a red bulb. A Tricky album. A spliff. In the hush between tracks, I could hear the wind moaning and the throaty barking of the dogs.

At some point, I mentioned that I was getting married.

Luca's eyebrows lifted. Who's the lucky girl?

Franca, I said.

Nice.

What do you mean, nice?

Nice body.

I gave him a look.

It's all right, he said. I haven't fucked her.

I did, Giotto said.

Luca put a hand on my arm. Giotto never fucked anyone. He's still a virgin.

Fuck you, Giotto said.

Half joking, half serious, they started a fight. Lurching one way across the floor, and then another, like an ungainly ball made of two people. Someone's foot went through a Scarface poster. The lamp toppled over. The red bulb popped.

Later, I crept past the great-aunt, who was unconscious in her armchair, her sunglasses still on, her mouth a black hole in her face. A breakfast show on TV. People in primary colors, smiling.

A brand-new day.

I stood on the gravel outside the house. The dogs were quiet. High above me was the village, mounted on its pedestal of trees. I heard the distant whine of someone sawing through a log. My heart was bouncing like a bee trapped in a jar. I had no idea what I'd taken.

When I walked into my parents' house, my father was sitting at the kitchen table, where I had left him nine hours earlier. The pomegranate was still in front of him, the two halves hollowed out.

Didn't you go to bed, Dad? I said.

Yes, I went to bed, he said. I couldn't sleep, though. All that wind and rain. He shifted in his chair. I'm sorry about everything.

I'm sorry too, I said.

I filled a glass with water and drank it down, then I filled the glass again. I hadn't realized how thirsty I was.

Turning back to my father, I told him I was off to bed. He nodded, but said nothing. Still, it was the closest we had been in years.

That weekend, I was invited to lunch by Franca's parents, Marcello and Silvana. It would be the first time I had seen them since Franca and I had decided to get married. Determined to make a good impression, I drove into Vasto on Saturday and bought an apple-and-lemon cake from an upmarket *pasticceria*. On Sunday morning, I showered and shaved, then I put on my only suit, which was dark-blue. I even wore a tie. When I arrived at Franca's parents' apartment, I handed the dessert to Silvana. She pretended to be cross with me for spending too much money, though I could tell that she was pleased. Marcello shook my hand, then asked if somebody had died. Before I could work out what he was referring to, he grinned and mock-punched me on the shoulder. I'm joking, he said. It's your suit. Franca came and took me by the arm. Don't pay any attention to him, she said.

She introduced me to Silvana's sister, Antonella, and Antonella's husband, Ciro. They had driven over from Lanciano. I also met Marcello's cousin, Alessio. He was as celebrated for his honey as my father was for his tomatoes. I stepped out onto the balcony, where Harry French was smoking a Toscano. When he saw me, he came over and embraced me. You finally got round to it, he said. I was worried that you never would.

So you think it's the right thing to do? I said.

You and Franca? he said. It's written in the stars. He looked past me, into the room. Where are Giancarlo and Gabriella?

My mother has a fever, and my father decided to stay at home to care for her.

Harry nodded. Does he approve of the marriage?

You know what he's like, I said. He doesn't really approve of anything I do.

Harry's face clouded over, and I searched for something that would cheer him up.

He likes Franca, though, I said.

Good. Harry stubbed out his cigar. That's good.

Lunch was a success, with everybody talking and drinking and laughing. The only awkward moment came towards the end. As Silvana was serving slices of the dessert that I had brought, Marcello turned to her and asked if she had heard about Enzo.

She paused. Which Enzo?

Pierozzi.

I glanced at Franca, but she kept her eyes on her plate.

What about him? Silvana said.

Marcello told her that Enzo had been in a pile-up on the *autostrada*.

Did you go? she said.

In the ambulance, she meant.

Marcello shook his head. It was way north of here, near Ancona.

Harry wanted to know if Enzo was all right. The moment that Harry spoke it struck me as unusual that Silvana hadn't asked. She'd had every chance to, and since Enzo and her husband were friends she must surely know him better than Harry did.

He wasn't hurt at all, not even a scratch. Marcello was laughing in disbelief.

Charmed life, Harry said.

Marcello nodded. His car's a write-off, though.

A silence fell, and I was hoping that nobody would mention my run-in with the tiger, but then Silvana spoke again.

He's one of those people who attract disaster.

Marcello's laughter stopped abruptly. What do you mean by that, Silvà?

Silvana's head was lowered, but I saw a smile ghost across her face.

Things keep happening to him, she said. Things go wrong.

There was an odd chill at the table, as if we were eating outdoors and the sun had suddenly gone in. I thought someone should say something.

Who's Enzo? I asked.

Enzo Pierozzi, Marcello said. He's a friend. But he answered me absentmindedly, and without even a glance in my direction. He was still looking at his wife. Her remarks had troubled him.

I was quiet, thinking of the man in the hard hat. His absolute confidence. His absolute disdain. The black hair glistening on his wrists and arms.

I don't think I know him, I said.

He and Marcello, Alessio said. They've known each other since forever.

Marcello was nodding enthusiastically.

Given Pierozzi was an old friend of Franca's father, it was hardly surprising that she had wanted to keep what she had done a secret, but it made me uncomfortable, since it seemed that I was also now, through no fault of my own, involved in the deceit.

Gino, Silvana said, are you all right?

She looked at me searchingly with her dark eyes. Did she already know about her daughter's affair? Had she guessed? Perhaps her curious observations about Pierozzi, which almost amounted to wishes or prophecies, I felt, were her way of dealing with the fact that she was in possession of knowledge which she would rather not have had, and which she couldn't share, for fear of how her husband might react. Or was it possible that she had learned of the affair just now, by reading my thoughts? Silvana had always been uncannily intuitive, and her supernatural powers were never more in evidence than in that moment. The room had fallen silent, and everybody's eyes had turned in my direction. I knew I couldn't lie to Silvana, or try to change the subject. I would tell the truth, I decided—but a different truth, one that would obscure what I had been thinking, one she couldn't take issue with or see through.

Things going wrong, I said. I used to be one of those people.

It seemed almost perverse to be allying myself with Pierozzi, since he was the last person I would have wanted to be associated with, and yet I felt it gave what I was saying real credence. Certainly I had Marcello's attention now. But Silvana saved me from going into detail by reaching across the table and putting her hand on mine.

No need to dwell on the past, she said. That's water under the bridge. And anyway, she went on with a smile, you're family now.

Well, not quite, Marcello said.

Everybody laughed more than the joke warranted, possibly out of relief that a potentially difficult conversation had been avoided.

I had given the impression that I was full of remorse for my behavior when I was younger. I had owned it in public, in front of my new family, the very side of me that they were concerned about, or suspicious of, and in doing so I had made it clear not only that I had changed, but also that I had acquired some self-knowledge, and that was due in no small part to Franca's influence—I didn't say as much, but that was the implication—and it felt so genuine, so authentic, that Silvana, for all her perspicacity, had fallen for it, and the people gathered round the table had fallen for it too, and as with all successful deceptions, there was even a sense in which I, the deceiver, had fallen for it myself.

Silvana left the room, and everybody started talking about the honey that Alessio had brought with him. The atmosphere shifted—sweetened, one might say— and finally, now that the danger had passed, I was able to risk another glance at Franca. Her eyes lifted, and there was a heat and an intensity about her look. I wasn't sure if she was grateful to me for acting as a decoy and distracting people from her secret, or if she was ashamed for having a secret in the first place—though it wasn't in her character, I thought, to feel shame. Whenever we touched on the subject of Pierozzi, she was straightforward and unapologetic. The affair hadn't turned out well, but she didn't regret it, and she didn't view it as a mistake, or even as risky or reckless behavior. She had done what she had done, and now it was over. But that didn't mean that she wanted her family to know about it. In fact, that was the last thing she wanted.

Silvana appeared with a bottle of prosecco and a tray of champagne flutes.

I believe we have something to celebrate, she said.

Marcello popped the cork, and once the prosecco had been poured he raised his glass.

To my daughter, Franca, and my future son-in-law, Gino, he said. Long life and happiness.


After that strange, almost tender encounter with my father, when I returned at dawn to find him sitting in the kitchen with the pomegranates, the tension in our home had eased. One evening, at dinner, I started telling my parents about La Peschiera, and how Franca and I had come to an arrangement with the owner of the property, her aunt Agnese.

Wasn't there a story about Agnese? My mother looked at my father, then at me. I don't know how much of it's true—or even if it's true at all. Her voice faltered.

Tell me, I said. Please.

She turned to my father. You tell it, Giancà.

He seemed reluctant, but he began. I don't know if you know the history, Gino, but it happened in the autumn of 1943, during a period of great political upheaval and confusion. Italy had just surrendered to the Allied forces, who had landed in the south, but Abruzzo was still occupied by the German army. Agnese was living at La Peschiera with her family. She had a fiancé called Leo. They were due to be married when she turned eighteen, in November of that year.

In September, my father went on, Agnese went missing. Local people organized search parties, combing the entire area—the woods, the farms, and the rivers—but she was nowhere to be found. Her family and friends were beside themselves, as you might imagine. Then, after three days, she turned up in a little church in Carunchio. She was lying near the altar, wrapped in a sheet. Her clothes were gone. At first, she couldn't talk, though she seemed to recognize those closest to her. When she regained the power of speech, she was at a loss to explain what had happened. She had no memory of those three days, none at all.

She married Leo in November, as planned, my father said. In June of the following year, she gave birth to a baby girl. He gave me a meaningful look. Not long afterwards, the rumors started.

I did a quick calculation. Because the baby was born nine months after she vanished, I said, not nine months after the wedding?

My father nodded, his expression grim.

How did Leo react? I asked.

With great dignity, my mother said.

That didn't stop people talking, my father said. People thought the Germans had something to do with it. By then, of course, the Germans had become the enemy.

There was no proof, though, I said.

None. My father shook his head, his eyes tired and haunted. I don't like repeating the story, he said, as most of it is probably just rumor, but if you're going to live there perhaps it's only right that you should know.

The following weekend, I drove out to La Peschiera with Franca. As yet, there was no electricity or running water, but we spent the day emptying the house of anything we didn't want. We burned the broken chairs and old, stained mattresses on the flat land at the back, and put the rest of the rubbish in black plastic bags, which we loaded into the boot of the car.

Towards the end of the afternoon, as we stood watching the flames, I told Franca what my parents had told me. She nodded. Apparently, the person behind the rumors was a young man who had loved Agnese, and had been rejected by her. It was done out of jealousy, and a desire for revenge. Agnese was bitter about it, and also mortified, of course, but she had no power in the situation. In those days, a reputation was everything, and hers was ruined. Some people even thought that she hadn't been abducted at all, but had chosen to elope with a German soldier, and that she was only pretending not to remember what had happened. In the end, after an uncomfortable year or two, the young couple decided to move to Casalbordino, where no one knew them.

But she's on her own now, I said.

Her husband died young, in his forties, Franca said, and the daughter lives in America. I think they speak on the phone sometimes.

That evening, we drove back in the last of the light, our clothes and hair smelling of the fire. As we reached a junction, our track joining a larger, more well-trodden road at an acute angle, Franca leaned forwards. This is where Agnese disappeared, she said. Or rather, this is the last thing she remembers, being here.

I stopped the car. To the west, the land rose to a low, rounded hill, with olive trees giving way to dense woods. To the east, where there were more olive trees, the ground dropped away into a valley. The sun almost gone, but a blue sky overhead.

Utter stillness.

And no one knows what happened, I said, even now?

Even now, she said.

I sensed a flickering, as if a bird had taken wing at the very edge of my field of vision. Then I shifted into gear and drove on.

September was unusual that year, with low temperatures and rain for days on end, but in October the weather heated up, and there were times when it felt like the height of summer.

One warm weekend, I was clearing the ground around the fig trees when my father came round the side of the house with Franca.

Look who's here, she said.

My father had a sheepish expression, as though he had been caught doing something embarrassing. It must be the effect that Franca has on him, I thought. He had always had a soft spot for her, perhaps. It had been his idea, after all, for me to look her up.

You didn't tell me you were dropping in, I said.

I was over this way, he said. Thought I'd come and see how things were going.

Franca asked if he would like some water. I'm afraid that's all we have, she told him.

He smiled quickly, almost painfully.

Water's fine, he said.

Franca vanished into the house.

My father stood gazing out over the wooded gulley in his blue work trousers and his faded, short-sleeved shirt. His big hands hung against his thighs, the fingers twitching.

I forgot to tell you, he said. I know this house. I came here once, with Harry.

Really?

It was when he was first in the area, looking for a place to buy. He liked it, actually. Agnese wouldn't sell it to him, though.

Franca appeared with a glass of water. My father thanked her and took a sip, then turned his back on the view and surveyed the house, the look on his face appraising, but also dubious.

I told him it was just as well, he said. It was too remote. Too out of the way. He should look for something in the village. He took another sip of the water. He listened to me, in the end.

But it's all right for me and Franca? I said.

You're still young. It's different for you.

There was a certain logic to what he was saying. All the same, I wondered if my decision to move to the country had come as a relief to him. He had played no part in my decision—I hadn't consulted him or been influenced by him—but if I was living out here, in the middle of nowhere, he wouldn't have to deal with me on a daily basis. I would be less of a burden to him. Had I unknowingly played into his hands?

What do I remember of those days?

Lying naked on a blanket after making love, the kitchen window and the door wide open. A weekend in October. The sun slanting through the fig trees, across our legs. The next time I looked, our bodies were in shadow, and I had the feeling that someone had peered in at us while we were sleeping.

Are you awake? I said.

She sat up and rubbed one eye with the back of her hand, seeming for those few moments much younger than she was.

I was dreaming, she said.

What did you dream?

You were walking away from me, across a piece of rough ground. It was like the ground at the back of the house, only bigger. I was calling your name. I needed you for some reason. I was scared. You didn't hear me, though. You just kept walking. She gave me an accusing look, as if it was something I had done, and I owed her an explanation.

I would never do that, I said.

But she still had the accusing look. I hadn't succeeded in convincing her.

It was a dream, Franca, I said. I didn't actually do it.

And you won't, will you.

No. I promise.

What else do I remember?

Sanding and plastering, and painting the walls and doors and windows, but also eating ripe figs off the trees, and drinking wine out of jam jars, and chasing each other, laughing, through empty rooms. In hindsight, it seemed like a lull, like the warm air that moves in ahead of a weather front, something blissful and mysterious, and not entirely to be trusted, not wholly real. At the same time, a new life was beginning, a life that neither of us had ever dared to hope for, or been able to imagine.

Our wedding took place in January, on a day of bright winter sun. The night before, I serenaded Franca with a group of friends. I sang the Neapolitan classic, "Comme facette mammeta"—*When your mother made you*—as the words seemed uncannily appropriate.

> *And to make that lovely mouth*
> *There were other things she added*
> *Want to know what she put in?*
> *A basket filled to the brim*
> *With strawberries from the garden*

After I had finished singing, I climbed a ladder to her parents' second floor apartment with a bunch of orange lilies, which was Franca's favorite flower, and after I had taken her in my arms and kissed her I turned to the crowd gathered below and said, That's probably the most dangerous thing I've ever done, and someone said, I seriously doubt that, and everybody laughed.

We had hoped to keep things simple, but our families thought otherwise. There was the full wedding mass, and the satin-and-organza dress. There was the choreographed kiss as we left the church, and the prosecco that we toasted each other with in the back of a Piaggio Ape as we were paraded through the village, and the pair of white doves that we released into the air on our arrival at the restaurant. There was the lunch for one hundred and fifty guests. There was also the moment, in the early evening, when we were invited to dance in front of everyone. As the Fred Buscaglione song began and I held Franca tightly against me, the two of us half-blinded by the spotlight's silver glare, I told her that I was grateful for the effort that our parents had made, and for the expense that they had gone to, but I would be glad when this part was over. She put her mouth close to my ear. My face aches from all the smiling, she said. I laughed, then told her that we would soon be on our own again. She pressed herself closer still and murmured the words that she had murmured on the alley steps in August. *I'm yours. I always have been.* As we kissed again and the applause burst through the elaborately decorated room, Fred

Buscaglione went on singing about the strange game of destiny, and a place made just for lovers, and how his path through life was no longer filled with sorrow.

That night, in our hotel in Vasto Marina, I dreamed I was in a car with three people who I didn't know. The woman sitting in the back with me was about my age, as were the two men in front. The man in the passenger seat had sandy-colored hair, and was built like a boxer, with a strong neck and wide shoulders. As we drove north, up the Adriatica, a service station appeared ahead of us, and the driver pulled in, saying that we needed petrol. It was early evening, not quite dark, the forecourt deserted except for a group of people over by the pumps. They wore black leather jackets and heavy boots. One of the men glanced in my direction, and I recognized him immediately.

Pierozzi.

Don't talk to them, I said to the three people in the car. Don't even look at them.

But it was too late. Some of the group were already moving towards us. They seemed to think that we'd been staring at their women.

The sandy-haired man spoke to them through his open window. Stare at your women? he said. Why would we bother? Then he made another remark, which was even more insulting.

I told you not to talk to them, I said.

He wasn't listening—and anyway, the gang had already surrounded us. Two of them gripped the roof and began to rock the car from side to side.

Pierozzi stepped closer, and he was leering at me through the window, a petrol pump in his right hand.

Super 95 or diesel? he said.

Without waiting for an answer, he sprayed petrol all over the outside of the car.

They're going to set fire to us, I cried.

There was a crash, and bits of glass struck my face and landed on my clothes. Hands reached into the car, grabbing the young woman. One of them had her by the hair. They were trying to pull her out through the broken window. She was screaming.

I woke suddenly, not knowing where I was. My T-shirt was wet. A soft, rushing sound came from beyond the window. You're in Vasto Marina, I told myself. I looked at the young woman sleeping peacefully beside me. No, no, I murmured. I couldn't believe in it. It was as if the scene in the petrol station was still happening, or was about to happen, and the scene in the hotel, with the sea view and the king-size bed and the white dress draped over the chair, was all a dream. I went into the bathroom and closed the door. I turned on the light. I stared at myself in the mirror.

Dopey, I muttered. Fucking Dopey.

Perhaps I was still drunk from the wedding party.

I took off my T-shirt and dropped it on the floor, then I reached for one of the fluffy, cream-colored towels. As I was drying myself, the door opened, and Franca walked in.

What time is it? She was yawning.

I've no idea, I said.

Are you all right?

Her sleepy face, her long brown hair. The old vest that she liked to wear in bed. She was ugly, and she was beautiful, and I couldn't tell the two apart. How I love her, I thought. How like a dream it is, after all.

I had a nightmare, I said.

She pushed herself against me, her arms around my waist, her head under my chin.

I'm here, she said. I'm real.

Tell me again.

I'm here, she said. We're married. I'm your wife.

I stroked her hair, but didn't speak.

You're in a new place, she said, somewhere that's not familiar. That's all it is. She took my hand. Come back to bed.


We moved into La Peschiera at the end of that month. My father's wedding present came as a surprise. I had thought that he would give us something that would appeal to him—a pomegranate tree, or a tomato plant. Instead, he bought a boiler and arranged to have it installed. You'll be needing hot water, he told us. It's a long time till the spring.

For the first few weeks we lived downstairs. The fireplace in the kitchen was our only source of heat. The room next to the kitchen became a temporary bedroom. We tried to keep the fire going through the night. If it went out, which it sometimes did, we found ourselves in a darkness that was absolute. Outside were all kinds of noises that we didn't recognize, and couldn't explain. Wolves had been sighted in the south of Abruzzo. What if there were other, more unearthly forces, though? Sometimes I worried that Franca might disappear, as Agnese had. I would speak into the pitch black. Are you there? I would say. Are you still there? She would reach out and touch me, to reassure me, or else she would murmur sleepily, Yes, I'm here.

We quickly established a routine. At weekends, we often had to see our families, but we also worked on the house. There was still so much to do. Sometimes, on a Saturday, we had lunch with Pasquale, or if we felt like a change we would go to a restaurant in the woods near Fraine and order pizza. On weekday mornings, we drove into work together, exactly as Franca had imagined. After turning past an isolated farmhouse with an old oak at the front, we sped down a long, curving road, the land falling away dramatically on both sides. Commanding the view, but buried in a tangle of wild figs and brambles, was a ruined villa with a faded pink facade. Further on, when the ground leveled out, the trees closed in on us, and then we joined the Isernia road, heading east, towards the coast. I would drop Franca first, then I would continue on to Vasto. Since I wasn't supposed to leave the office before five thirty, Franca would either work late or she would wait for me in Toni's bar, which was a short walk from her building.

One evening in March, I was delayed—the accounts at Lidl were being audited—and when I called to let Franca know, there was no reply. She must already have left the office. It was almost half past six by the time I parked outside Toni's bar. As I locked the car, I glanced round, expecting her to be sitting by the window, but the table was unoccupied. I crossed the street and pushed the glass door open. Franca was seated in the corner, facing away from me. Opposite her was a man I didn't know. When the man saw me, he gave me a smile that was easy and relaxed. By the time I reached their table, he was already on his feet.

You must be Franca's husband, he said, shaking my hand. She was wondering where you'd got to.

He seemed to be saying more than he needed to.

You're so late. By now, Franca was also on her feet, but I was still looking at the man. He was tall, with a long neck. All his teeth showed when he smiled.

I'm Michele, he said.

Gino, I said.

He was smiling again. I know.

Are you a work colleague?

No. But I live nearby. Just down the street. He pointed through the window.

Where have you been? Franca asked me.

I'm sorry, I said. I was held up. I tried to call you, but you'd already left.

The man reached for his beer and finished it.

I should be going, he said.

He nodded to both of us, then left the bar. I watched him through the window as he looked both ways, then hurried across the street.

Michele.

He's one of my regulars. Toni was speaking to me from behind the counter. He's all right.

I asked Franca if she had met the man before.

I don't know, she said. I mean, he might have been here, and I might have said hello, but I really don't remember.

Tonight you got talking, though?

I was looking around, wondering where you'd got to, and he asked if I'd like a drink. I said I'd buy my own, but somehow, yes, we started talking. I didn't mind. It made the time go faster.

Next time I'll call you here. I looked at Toni. That's okay, isn't it?

Of course, he said.

Eyes lowered, he wiped the counter with an old cloth.

We left soon after.

As we took the curve that led up to the Isernia road, rain swept in from the south, as if someone was crossing out the land that lay in front of us with a lead pencil. In my head, too, there was a vicious scribbling. I was thinking of the expression on the man's face just before he saw me. He was so absorbed by Franca—either by what she was saying or by how she looked—that it was a wonder he had noticed me at all. There was a side to him that was like an antenna, perhaps, alert to the possibility of my arrival. If that was the case, though, it would seem to suggest some indiscretion on his part. But it could be that I was reading far too much into that one split second. Better, probably, to focus on what Toni had said. *He's all right.*


It was the wettest spring that anybody could remember. One night towards the end of the month, while I was preparing dinner, there was a knock on the door. Franca and I exchanged a look. Who could be visiting so late, and in such weather?

When Franca opened the door, Harry was standing outside, rain dripping from the wide brim of his hat. He had a large brown-paper package under one arm. Franca told him to come in.

This place isn't easy to find, he said, as he took off his coat and hat. I almost gave up.

I thought you were here once before, I said.

That was fifteen years ago, he said, and your father was driving.

When did you get back? Franca asked.

Yesterday. He put the package on the kitchen table. That's your wedding present. I'm sorry I couldn't make it over in January. Family commitments. He gave us one of his weird, grim smiles.

Franca tore off the brown paper. Inside, sealed in plastic, were two king-size sheets, four pillowcases, and a duvet cover, all white.

Egyptian cotton, she said, reading the label.

Only the best for you two, Harry said.

A few minutes later, he tried to leave, but we persuaded him to stay for dinner.

Sitting at the table after the meal, I turned to Franca and said that Harry's present reminded me of Agnese. Harry wanted to know who Agnese was. She's the woman who refused to sell you this house, I said. He said that he had never met her. I told him the story of her disappearance, and how she turned up in a church in Carunchio, wearing nothing but a sheet. Harry thought that most people had times in their lives that were like that—not as extreme, perhaps, but episodes or periods that they had either forgotten, or wished they could forget.

Even you? I said.

With me, it lasted for years, he said, then he looked round at the room. You've done wonders with this place.

Later, after Franca had gone to bed, we sat by the fire with glasses of red wine, smoking the duty-free Camels that Harry had brought with him.

The time you want to forget, I said, did it happen when you were living in Hong Kong?

He sighed. I come all the way out here in the rain with your wedding present, and what do I get? A grilling. Like I'm some kind of criminal.

I grinned. You got dinner too. And anyway, I thought we were friends. If you can't confide in a friend, who can you confide in?

He put his glass down, but kept his eyes on it. The color of the wine in the firelight seemed to have him hypnotized.

I was unfaithful to my wife, he said, and she found out. Our marriage was over in five seconds. His fierce black eyebrows lifted, then dropped again. She wanted to kill me—or have me killed. She told me she might even pay someone to kill me. You could do that in Hong Kong. It didn't even cost that much. He gave me a tight grin that was like a wince. Instead, she moved back to the UK. And it was strange, because I spent the next seven years behaving as if I wanted to die. It was almost as if I was trying to carry out her wish for her. As if it was some kind of prophecy that had to be fulfilled.

I don't understand, I said. What did you do?

He shook his head. Crazy things.

Like what?

He told me about a night he went out drinking with people from the office. It got late, and they went home, but somehow he didn't think of doing that. It was winter, and a thick fog had descended on the city, soaking up the light from all the brightly colored neon signs. Visibility was down to almost nothing. After wandering from bar to bar, he found himself near Kowloon Bay. Four in the morning. No sign of dawn as yet. He decided to lie down in the middle of a main road and see if anything ran him over.

I stared at him, wide-eyed.

He spread his hands. Obviously, I'm still here.

You're right, I said. That's crazy.

It was uncanny, he went on. Nothing came. After about ten minutes, I got to my feet and walked to the side of the road. It was only then that a truck went past. Huge thing. Eighteen wheels. He lit another Camel. I wasn't always that self-destructive, but I did a lot of stupid things. He looked at me steadily, through the smoke. I'm not proud of it, Gino. That's not why I'm telling you.

I reached for my glass and drank. Outside, the rain had stopped, and a wind was rushing through the fig trees.

Of course, you've had your moments too, Harry said.

I nodded. Everybody knew the stories.

Your father was so upset, Harry went on. He used to ask me what he had done wrong.

What did you tell him?

I gave him an honest answer. I said I didn't know. I also said that when it comes to children everybody makes mistakes. Leaning forwards, Harry threw his cigarette into the fire. Maybe you were lucky that it happened when it did. When you were still so young. I was almost fifty. He smiled and shook his head, then he studied the palm of his right hand. Sometimes I think I needed to go through all that just to get to where I am now.

You have to survive it, though, I said. You might not have survived. One truck is all it would have taken. One car.

I know, it was a period of madness. That's how I look at it. But it's over now. I'm calm.

After Harry took his leave, I climbed the stairs and stood in the darkened corridor. I thought of waving, but he didn't look up as he crossed the rough ground at the back of the house in his black coat and his wide-brimmed hat, his head and shoulders thrust forwards, into the wind. If he was someone I was seeing for the first time, how would I have described him? I doubted that "calm" would be the word that I came up with.

Franca was awake when I climbed into bed.

Has he gone? she asked sleepily.

I nodded. He just left.

Such a lovely present.

I know. He's very kind.

I thought I heard the far-off drone of Harry's car. He would be driving along the country roads, his hat pulled down over his narrow eyes, his mouth set in a straight line. He was out there, in the dark, on a quest for calmness. It kept eluding him, though. Or perhaps the calmness he was looking for didn't actually exist. Perhaps it was like the end of the rainbow—a place that's sought-after, but always out of reach.

Franca pulled me closer.

You feel different, I said. Your breasts.

What about them?

They were fuller, I thought. Heavier. Almost swollen.

You still like them? she said.

I smiled, but didn't answer.

The sex we had that night was like being caught up in a typhoon or a tornado. I was whirled right out of myself. All at once I was high up and far away. Whole landscapes passed beneath me. Forest, mountain ranges. Desert sands. I covered great distances with no effort.

When I returned to the room, the window, walls, and door invisible, I still had the sense of being weightless and aloft, though gradually my body lowered itself down into the bed, and then I sank even further, into sleep.

The next day, on our way home from work, Franca turned to me in the car.

I took a test, she said. I'm pregnant.

I couldn't believe how happy I was. Franca couldn't believe it either. She seemed to have doubts, and she was surprised that I didn't have them too. But I didn't. My happiness was instant, thoughtless. Undeniable.

You don't think it has come too soon? she said.

We were sitting in front of the house, at the small round metal table I had bought from a secondhand shop in Vasto. Spring sunlight slanted across her. It was a Saturday.

Too soon? I said.

We haven't had much time together, she said, by ourselves.

I moved my chair closer and put an arm around her shoulders. You, me, the house, the baby—it's all part of our luck. It's not something we should think of questioning.

She looked down at her belly, which was still flat.

I'm having a baby, she said.

There was a freshness to her skin that morning, and I wondered later, as I drove into Carunchio to pick up some groceries, if that explained why the man in Toni's bar had been so captivated by her. Perhaps he had sensed the bloom in her, the inner glow.

At first, we kept it a secret, and then, in May, when the doctor said it was safe to tell people, I went to see my parents. I was looking forward to saying the words out loud. *I'm going to be a father.* They seemed to increase my importance and to lessen it, both at the same time. Someone would be relying on me, someone who I would readily make sacrifices for, someone whose existence would be worth more than mine.

My mother was in the kitchen, preparing artichokes. When I told her the news, she reached up and put a hand against my cheek.

I'm very happy for you.

Later, as we sat at the table, she said she hadn't seen this coming. She had hoped for it, of course—what mother wouldn't?—but she had never expected it.

You didn't think we'd have children? I said.

I didn't know if you wanted them, she said. Not everyone wants children. Also, you're still so young. You only just got married! She sipped her coffee. Have you told your father?

Not yet, I said. I wanted to tell you first.

I asked her if she would tell him for me, but she thought I ought to do it myself. It was one of those moments when I longed for her to intervene. How could she ignore all the difficulties I'd had with him? Why would things go any differently this time? In the light of that, couldn't she have taken on the task, or at least offered some words of caution or advice? But no, she persisted in seeing him through her own eyes. She was in denial, perhaps, or else she was complicit. I'd always seen my mother as an innocent, but it might not have been as simple as that.

I found my father where she told me he would be, at the bottom of the hill, between two rows of peppers. He was bent over, securing the stalk of a plant to an upright cane, his bald spot brown from the sun.

Still bent over, he glanced sideways and upwards.

Gino, he said, what brings you here?

Why did I always feel as if he would rather that I hadn't appeared? I went on, though, regardless.

Good news, I said.

He straightened up, rubbing one hand against the other. As always, he was wearing his blue work trousers and his faded shirt.

I looked away from him, into the sky. I'm going to be a father.

A father? he said. Well, well. He lowered his eyes and wrapped a hand around the back of his neck. You think you're ready? It's a big responsibility.

Did you hesitate, I said, before you had me?

No, he said.

His look was wary suddenly, and I thought I knew what he was thinking. *But I'm not you, am I?* The village lay behind him—the square tower of the church, the whirling rooks, and Palmoli visible beyond, on a distant blue-green ridge.

I scuffed at the earth with the side of my boot.

Only a few months before, at Sunday lunch with Franca's family, I had been encouraged to view my waywardness as a thing of the past, but now, in the presence of my father, it rose up inside me once again, as irresistible as ever, and I found myself wondering if it might be a pattern of behavior that he had imposed on me, if it might actually be his idea, his creation. Perhaps it was even something he needed, for his own sense of self. He couldn't be who he was unless I was the opposite.

In our case, it was different, he told me. You came late in our lives. We had almost resigned ourselves, your mother and I, to being on our own.

I had come late, which wasn't necessarily better than never. In fact, it might have been worse.

Would you rather I hadn't come at all? I said.

Exasperation drew the air from him in a rush. That isn't what I was saying.

You know, when someone tells you that they're going to be a father, I said, when your own son tells you that, there's really only one response.

He looked at me, his impassiveness edged with uncertainty, as if he knew deep down that he was guilty of wrongdoing, but he seemed stubborn too, as my mother was. He wasn't about to let go of his view of me, not without some concrete evidence of change. And even then.

*How wonderful,* I said. *Congratulations. You must be thrilled.* Any of those would have done. What I don't need to hear is how I'm not cut out to have a child, how I'm not mature enough, how I'll only make a mess of it—

I was only saying—

Don't, I said. Please. Just don't.

We stared at each other for a moment, then I turned away and started back towards the house. He didn't try to stop me. He didn't even call my name.

As I climbed the hill, the dream that had poisoned my wedding night rose into my head again, the feeling that terrible events awaited me, and there was nothing I could do, and I cursed my father under my breath for constantly reminding me of my inadequacy and my shortcomings, and not for the first time in my life I wished him dead and gone.

At the beginning of June, when Franca was three months pregnant, I took her to Nemi for the strawberry festival. Since we had never been away together before, not even after our wedding, we decided to think of it as our honeymoon. We left early on Saturday morning, the sun already hot, the world a dome of silver and bright blue. As we drove west, through the mountains, I talked about the village, which was next to a volcanic lake known as Diana's Mirror. According to the Romans, the goddess lived in the woods on the north shore, and they had built a temple to her. Not much was left now, only ruins. In the past, though, pregnant women would journey to the temple to seek Diana's blessing. She wasn't just the goddess of the hunt. She was the goddess of childbirth as well.

But we're already blessed, Franca said.

They would also go there to thank her, I said, if she granted them fertility.

So you think we should thank her too? Her voice had an edge to it—not quite scathing, but close enough.

I looked across at her.

I mean, do you believe all that, she said more gently, about blessings and thanksgiving?

You don't have to, if you don't feel like it, I said. It was only an idea.

She put her feet on the dashboard and turned her head towards the window. Well, I suppose it can't do any harm.

You know, you should really fasten your seat belt, now there are two of you.

She seemed to consider arguing the point, then she smiled to herself and pulled the belt across her body and clicked it into place.

You're going to be a good father, she said.

I had booked our lodgings long in advance, before I knew Franca was pregnant, and then I had called ahead, a few days prior to our departure, to let the proprietor, Onofrio, know that it was our honeymoon. When we arrived in Nemi in the early afternoon, we found him in a café, playing cards. A man of about seventy, dressed in a worn gray suit, he led us across the main street, then down a damp, dead-end alley that smelled of cats. Franca looked at me as if to say, What have you got us into? Onofrio turned the key in a door, then stepped aside, allowing Franca to go first, but she stopped on the threshold, one hand lifting to her mouth. The room was huge and cool, with dark beams on the ceiling and a tile floor. There was a double bed with a carved wooden headboard and a chaise longue upholstered in gold fabric. On a writing desk, propped against a bottle of prosecco and a wicker basket of strawberries, was a quaint card with a picture of a bride and groom on the front.

I had the room cleaned yesterday, Onofrio told us, from top to bottom.

It's beautiful, Franca said. Thank you.

Onofrio nodded. I'll be next door, if you need anything. You only have to ask.

When the old man had gone, Franca picked up the card.

How did he know? she said.

I shrugged. Someone must have told him.

A few seconds passed, then my straight face crumpled, and she realized I had played a trick on her. She mock-punched me on the shoulder, then moved across the room. I followed her out onto the terrace, which was cloaked in jasmine, and there was the lake, far below, a single cloud suspended on its smooth blue surface. On the other side, and poised on the lip of the crater, was a village called Genzano di Roma, though I noticed Onofrio had refused to name it, referring to it dismissively as "that place over there."

We spent our first afternoon in bed, drinking the prosecco and eating the strawberries.

They taste as good as I remember, I told Franca, but not as good as you.

Are you sure? she said.

Nowhere near.

She smiled lazily, then kissed me.

Sounds drifted through the open window. The clatter of plates in a nearby restaurant, a child calling for his mother. Someone practicing a tarantella on the accordion. We must have dozed. When the sun had almost set, I looked across at Franca. She was lying on her back with the sheets pushed down to her waist, one arm draped over her eyes.

This isn't so bad, is it? I said.

I'm not leaving, she murmured. Not ever.

That evening, on our way to dinner, we found On- ofrio sitting on a chair outside his house. He asked if we had heard about the two enormous barges that used to be moored on the lake. They had been built by Caligula, he said. One had been devoted to the wor- ship of Diana. The other had been used exclusively for pleasure. After the emperor's assassination, the float- ing palaces were scuttled, and they lay undisturbed on the bottom of the lake for almost two thousand years. Towards the end of the 1920s, Mussolini engineered their recovery by having the whole lake drained. The barges were subsequently housed in a museum. Only a few years later, however, the museum—and the barges—were destroyed by a German bomb. After all that time in the dark, Onofrio said, where they were safe. He shook his head. For me, they're still down there, somehow.

We looked for a place to eat on the main street, but it was a Saturday, the night before the festival, and everything was fully booked, so we drove to Lake Al- bano. Fifteen minutes away by car, Albano was twice the size of Nemi, and there were more restaurants to choose from, some of them built right on the water. We found a table without any trouble.

As we were finishing our dinner, a woman came over. She apologized for disturbing us, but she wanted to offer her congratulations. She wore her white hair in a chignon and spoke with a foreign accent. A ruby glinted on her left hand.

Congratulations? Franca said. What for?

The woman smiled at her. You know what for.

Franca stared at the woman, but the woman wasn't discouraged in the slightest.

How many months? she asked.

About three, Franca said. But how could you tell? It doesn't show.

She was looking at her belly.

Not there, the woman said. It's in your face.

That's a lovely ring, I told her.

She glanced down at the ruby on her finger. It was an eighteenth birthday present from my grandfather. He died soon afterwards.

Franca put her hand on mine. It reminds me of that story you told me about Venus and Adonis.

I know that story, the woman said. The drops of blood that turned into strawberries.

Or maybe into rubies, I said.

The woman smiled again.

She told us that she had lost the ring once, while she was at the beach. She reported it to the police, but never dreamed that she would see it again. To her astonishment, a young man found it and handed it in. Her grandfather had purchased the ruby in Mogok, which made it rare and precious, but the ring also had enormous sentimental value. She had invited the young man to her villa, thinking to offer him a reward. He told her that would not be necessary. For him, he said, just knowing the ring had been returned to its rightful owner was a reward in itself. At that moment, the woman's granddaughter appeared. She had been for a swim in the pool and was drying her hair with a towel as she walked back through the olive grove. The woman introduced her granddaughter to the young man. They fell in love, and now, as it happened, they were expecting their first baby.

Like us, Franca said.

Like you, the woman said, then she turned to me. You see? Things have come full circle.

She wished us well, then left.

After dinner, we bought ice creams and went for a stroll along the lake. It was still early in the season, and the lidos hadn't opened yet, but the sun loungers were already laid out in rows, their pale umbrellas rolled up for the night and standing on one leg, like herons. There were other couples out walking, and also some young men on their own, their eyes and teeth glowing in the darkness. The air felt softer than in Abruzzo, almost drowsy, and the lake had a presence, though it wasn't moving. There was scarcely a ripple, even where it met the land, the lamps along the shore precisely mirrored in the motionless black water. Though this was a different lake, I couldn't help remembering what Onofrio had said about Caligula's barges. *For me, they're still down there.* I shivered at the thought.

Can you hear music? Franca said.

We had stopped outside a pair of high wrought-iron gates, one of which had been left ajar. At the end of the drive was a decaying palazzo. Gold light blazed from its many windows. Intrigued, we moved closer. On the ground floor was a kind of ballroom, with double doors that stood open to the night. An old-fashioned dance band had taken the stage, and the room was filled with couples dancing. The singer was dressed in a white tuxedo. He held the microphone daintily, as if it was a teacup, his little finger lifting into the air, and every now and then he flicked his black hair off his forehead, but wet-looking strands kept falling forwards into his eyes. All the men in the brass section were wearing sunglasses. As we lingered on the threshold, the singer noticed us and tilted his head sideways. He was inviting us to join the others on the dance floor.

Franca turned to me. Shall we?

I hung back. I had come of age in the clubs and raves of the nineties, and I had never learned formal dances like the foxtrot or the waltz. We would stick out. But Franca seemed to have no qualms at all.

Come on, she said. It'll be a laugh.

And suddenly we were in the thick of it, surrounded by people who were at least a generation older. We held each other tight and tried to move in time to the music. When I next looked at the singer, he gave me a wink, as if he had involved us in some sort of conspiracy or crime, and we had got away with it, but then his black hair and dark eyes began to crowd my vision, and the face I was seeing wasn't his, but that of Enzo Pierozzi. I knew I must be imagining it—the singer wasn't Pierozzi, how could he be?—and yet it was Pierozzi's voice that was in my ear, the voice I had heard in that concrete plant in Ortona, so soft and so insidious, and he wasn't singing anymore, even though the band was still playing and the people all around me were still dancing, he was speaking to me, his mouth against my ear, one eye closing in a wink and that little finger lifting off the mike, he was talking about Franca, what she liked to do in bed, and also what he had made her do, against her will, Franca lying naked in the Nettuno or the Sabrina, her arms reaching above her head, her belly pale, and Pierozzi standing over her, his wrists covered with black hair, and his voice too close to me, far too close, like something animal or bestial, his voice describing in great detail all the filthy things that they had done. My forehead hot and damp, my vision shutting down around the edges. The rasp of a saxophone. The cymbal's nonstop hiss. I felt I might be about to faint.

Franca noticed. Are you all right?

I have to leave, I murmured.

At that moment, luckily, the number ended, and as the dancers came to a standstill and applauded we slipped between them and out into the open air. Back on the road, beyond the iron gates, I found a bench and sat with my head between my knees.

Gino? She was looking down at me, concerned.

I told her I was fine. I just needed a moment. I had found it a bit stuffy, that was all.

The sweat cooled on my neck.

Behind us, in the palazzo, the band were starting up again. It was a number that I recognized. "Begin the Beguine." I didn't allow the singer's voice to reach me, only the lush strings, and the fidgety drums, and the brass section, which was carrying the tune.

Before the song was over, I stood up, and we walked back along the road, towards the car. The music faded. Franca knew me well enough to realize that whatever had happened was something I didn't want to think about.

Nothing needed to be said.


That night, we slept with the door to the terrace open. I couldn't see the lake from the bed, but I could sense that it was there. I thought I could smell the marsh cane and tall grasses at the water's edge. I could almost hear it, like something breathing out—a feathery, unending rush of air.

After all that time in the dark, Onofrio had said, where they were safe. In my mind, his musings about Caligula's pleasure boats were linked to the singer in the white tuxedo. Those whispered obscenities, which I didn't want to remember, but couldn't forget.

Why did Pierozzi keep appearing? It was as though he was haunting me—except that he wasn't insubstantial, the way a ghost would be. If anything, of the two of us, he seemed the more present, the more powerful.

The wind rose, and the jasmine on the terrace rustled.

Against all the odds, I slept deeply.

On the morning of the festival Franca woke me. Outside, I could already hear the babble of excited visitors.

I can feel him, Franca said. Like a buzzing—or a fizzing. Like a glass of Coca-Cola that has just been poured. She laughed, then took my hand and placed it on her belly. There.

You said "him."

It's a boy. I'm sure of it. Her head turned on the pillow, and she looked at me. I didn't know until that woman showed up at our table. She told me.

I don't remember her doing that.

She didn't tell me in the normal way. There were the words she said to us out loud, but then there were some other words. They were silent, and they went straight from her brain into mine.

Like telepathy, you mean?

I don't normally believe in that.

Me neither.

From that moment on, though, we thought of our baby as a boy, and we started trying to come up with a name for him. Franca suggested Annunzio, after her favorite uncle. He had kept sheep on the Maiella. After mulling it over, we decided that it didn't sound quite right. What about her father's father, Muzio? she said. He was a fisherman. He died at sea when he was only in his forties. But Muzio didn't sound right either. I came up with Guglielmo, my mother's father's name. He used to own a pizzeria in Termoli. No, we said again. Not right.

The festivities lasted the whole day, with processions through the village in the morning, a boisterous and slightly out-of-tune marching band leading the way, followed by the *fragolare*, women and young girls carrying baskets of strawberries and wearing white blouses, white aprons, and long red skirts, their flat white headdresses trailing shiny scarlet ribbons, and later, in the afternoon, men in red waistcoats and black trousers played accordions and tambourines while the women danced, and whenever there was a pause or a lull—if we were queueing for our *panini con la porchetta*, or sitting in a bar, waiting for our Campari Sodas to arrive—one of us would say a name. *Adriano. Alberto. Alessandro. Angelo. Antonio. Arcangelo. Armando. Carlo. Corrado. Dino. Domenico. Emanuele. Emiliano. Francesco. Franco. Giacinto. Gianfranco. Gianluca. Gianpaolo. Giovanni. Giuliano. Marco. Mario. Massimo. Maurizio. Nicola. Olindo. Orazio. Peppino. Rodolfo. Sergio. Stefano. Teodoro. Umberto. Valentino. Vittorio.* None of them seemed right. It was as if we were playing a game, but we were also serious. Our baby's name was out there, in the ether, ready to be discovered.

Towards midnight, as we stood on our terrace watching the fireworks burst from behind the trees on Piazza Roma and explode above the lake, Franca leaned into me, her arm around my waist.

I don't think we should force it with the names, she murmured. When one of us says it, we will know.

On Monday morning, we left our hotel at dawn. Franca in a short green dress and sandals, yawning. She hadn't wanted to get up, but I had forced her to. We would never have a chance like this again.

The previous evening, while she was in the shower, I had spoken to Onofrio, telling him that we wanted to visit the temple of Diana. Was it best to drive? He shook his head, making a disapproving noise with his tongue. You're young, he said. You can go on foot. It will only take you half an hour. You'll find the path at the north end of the village, just beyond the Porta di Nemus. He paused. There's only one problem. The temple is on land that's privately owned, and I don't believe it's open to the public. There must be some way in, I said. He looked at me sidelong, and though I thought I saw cunning and mischief in his eyes he wouldn't say anything else.

To begin with, the path was paved with smooth, worn stones. Further down, it became much more un-even. The cool shade, the huge, moss-covered boul-ders. The trees parting to reveal glimpses of the lake below. In Roman times, Onofrio had told me, women had walked down through the woods to find favor with Diana. Wildflowers would be woven into their hair, and they would be carrying lit torches. I decided to keep the knowledge to myself. It was enough that Franca had agreed to come with me.

On reaching level ground, we turned along a track lined with cypresses, then through an olive grove. The site of the temple was cordoned off, as Onofrio had warned that it might be, and the gate was padlocked, but we found a hole in the chain-link fence and we were able to scramble through.

Parts of the temple were out in the open, the rem-nants of its walls no more than ankle-high, like teeth set in the gums of the earth. On the far side, though, built up against the sheer, thickly wooded hill, was a row of tall archways or alcoves that were better preserved, and more secluded, their stonework draped in foliage. We pushed through the ferns and grasses, our legs soon wet with dew.

We came to a standstill in the shadow of the alcoves, beneath the overhanging trees.

Bending, Franca scratched behind one knee.

I think something bit me, she said

The undergrowth felt dense, exuberant. It seemed possible that the whole place could disappear, like the Aztec and Mayan cities that were lost for generations, swallowed by the jungle. I knelt in front of Franca, as I had knelt once before, in Casalbordino, on the narrow strip of pavement outside Agnese's house. I closed my eyes and pressed my face against her belly.

Are you in there? I whispered. I can't hear you.

Maybe he's still asleep, like all the sensible people. Franca's voice seemed to come from high above me, far away.

What about his heart? I said. If I listen hard enough, could I hear his heart?

Maybe. I don't know. She yawned again.

As I kneeled in front of her, the sun rose above the trees, and its light shone on my face, and on her belly, and I thought I sensed the buzzing or fizzing she had spoken of. Perhaps he was responding to the fall of brightness, the first hint of the day's heat.

You feel that, Franca?

The sun, you mean? She sounded drowsy, only half-awake.

My face was still pressed against her body, my arms curled round the back of her thighs, but I could feel the sun on my eyelids and on my cheek. In that moment, something came to me, the very thing that we had been searching for.

I think I know his name, I said.

You do?

Elio.

Elio, she said.

She looked away across the field of tall ferns and grasses. Her hair hung in loose waves past her shoulders. A pulse beat in her throat.

Yes, she said. That's it.

I stood up and we held each other.

*Elio.*

You didn't know it when you planned this trip, she told me later, when we were back in Nemi and sitting in a restaurant that overlooked the lake, but that was why we came. To find out that our baby was a boy. To learn his name.

I had no idea, I said. I didn't even know you were pregnant. All I was thinking about was our honeymoon.

And that would have been enough, she said. To be together, just the two of us. Her eyes followed a canoe out on the water, its wake a thin line in the blue. But this? This is so much more.

Our final morning. The terrace of our favorite café with its cream-colored parasols and its pools of shade. A plate of *tartine alle fragole* and two cappuccinos. The lake beyond the iron railing, opaque and flawless in the June sunlight.

A waiter came hurrying towards our table. I had the impression that he was frightened of us, and that he would rather have run in the opposite direction.

*Signore*, there's a call for you. You can take it by the cash till.

A call? I looked at Franca, and she shrugged.

When I picked up the phone, a woman said my name. The voice was pinched and quavery. It was a moment before I realized that it was my mother, Gabriella.

What's happened, my darling? I said. Is something wrong?

It's your father, she said.

She kept talking in that strange new voice, and she was crying too. I couldn't think of anything to say. The air in the café had turned to liquid. If I gestured, my hand made glassy ripples. A man in a linen jacket brushed past me with a smile on his face. I wanted to seize him by his lapels and shove him up against the wall. How could he go round smiling like that? Didn't he have the first idea? There were two worlds suddenly, one where I was and another one where he was, him and all the rest, and the hot blue day was still outside, just as it would have been if nobody had called me to the phone.

Franca's face lifted as I approached the table.

My father's dead, I said.

I sank down onto my chair, my hands on my knees, my throat constricted, dry.

He had gone out at five in the morning, I told her, as he often did, to tend to his land. Usually, he returned at seven. He always had the same breakfast. Bread, tomatoes, olive oil. Two cups of coffee.

At half past seven, there was still no sign of him. My mother began to worry. When eight o'clock struck and he had not returned, she went out to look for him. He was lying next to a tomato plant. He'd had a massive heart attack.

God, I'm so sorry, Franca said.

She rose from her chair and came round the table, then she bent over me and held me in her arms. Her hair fell all around me, keeping the world at bay, her hair which had waves in it, now that she was carrying our child.

I'm all right, I said. I'm fine.

Half an hour later, as we drove towards the *auto-strada*, I talked about how happy we had been in that village by the lake.

I don't think I've ever been happier, Franca said.

Nothing can wipe that out. I looked across at her. If you weren't here, I don't know what I'd do.

During the three-hour drive home, I kept thinking that I would break down, and that Franca would have to take the wheel, but the uncanny calmness I had felt on the café terrace, and later, in the room, while we were packing, was still uppermost. Around the edges of that feeling were subtle stabbings of frustration and regret. I hadn't been able to make my peace with my father, and now I never would. When I last saw him, he had implied that I wasn't ready for fatherhood, and I had turned my back on him and walked away. Had I been too hard on him, though? Had I expected too much? After all, I had let him down so often. There had been times when I had scared him too. He might even have feared for his life. How could he not have doubted me? How could he not have lost all faith?

I only have flashed or fractured images of that day. Cars parked on the drive, and down the hill. The sun's glare on their windscreens. A whip snake, black as licorice, flickering across the broken ground behind the house. Inside, in the gloom, my mother at the kitchen table, one hand against her brow, as if, without that support, her head might fall apart. I sat with her and held her in my arms, just as Franca had held me earlier. She said the same words over and over. *What am I going to do?* She felt smaller, as though my father's death had taken something from her, reduced her in some way. As though she might disappear, as he had. How quickly it all unravels, I thought. How quickly it is gone. A snarl of thunder in the late afternoon. A heavy shower. Then sun again, a world that shone. A double rainbow in the sky to the southeast.

When people pass away, they automatically turn into saints. According to everyone who knew him, my father had been perfect when he was alive. Imagine how perfect he became now he was dead! What a good husband he was, they said. What a good father. How generous he was, how loving. How wise. We won't see the likes of him again, the world's a poorer place, we'll miss him more than we can say. Throughout that day, and the days that came after, family and friends would approach me, and all I ever heard were eulogies and adulation. What about his failings, though? What about his inexhaustible capacity for disillusion and his unwillingness or inability to say, Well done? What about the burden of having to follow in his footsteps? Only in his garden, I imagined, was he ever free of disappointment. Only when he was on the land did he give praise. But what use was that to the rest of us? We couldn't share in it. We didn't even witness it. All we ever saw were the fruits of his labors—the tomatoes, the plums, the pomegranates, the peppers, the olives, the aubergines, the basil, the courgettes. In their flawlessness, they seemed to be finding fault with us. *This is the kind of thing that he expects. This is what makes him happy.*

Feeling as if the walls were closing around me, I went outside to get some air. It was evening. A cousin of my mother's—Mario, from Rimini—was standing on the terrace, smoking.

Cigarette? He offered me the packet.

I took one. Thank you.

He lit it for me, and we stood there, side by side, looking out into the dark. The trickle of water in the drainpipes. A car's headlights on the hill.

You're the head of the family now, he said. Your mother's going to need you.

I know. I drew on the cigarette and blew the smoke out slowly.

When's the baby due?

December.

He glanced at me sidelong. You must be very proud.

It's what I needed, I said, even before all this.

One life departs, another arrives. He sighed, then brushed a few flakes of ash off the front of his shirt. Seventy-six. He shook his head. He should have lived much longer.

I murmured something, then dropped my cigarette and crushed it with my shoe.

He glanced at me again. You didn't always get on, did you.

We weren't very alike, I said. He found that difficult.

I saw that Mario needed to hear something different, something a little more encouraging.

We had some good moments, I said.

He put a hand on my shoulder.

Of course you did, he said. Try to remember those.

That night, I woke suddenly. Steel-colored moonlight filled the room. Franca was asleep beside me, in her white vest. Instead of returning to La Peschiera, we had decided to stay with my mother, at least for the time being, but we had been so tired when we went to bed that we had forgotten to close the shutters. The dream I had woken from had left only traces of itself. A lake with no water in it, and me up to my ankles in mud and slime. Then I was in La Peschiera, but the rooms were derelict. Smashed tiles on the floor, the roof half gone. A skinned animal lying on the grass outside. Smoke drifting, an uprooted tree. Like a war zone.

The previous evening, there had been a vigil for my father in the large room next to the front door. He lay in an open coffin in his brown Sunday suit, his hands folded on his belly, a rosary artfully threaded through his fingers. There was a disdainful curve to his nos-trils, as if he could smell something he didn't like. My mother sat beside him, at the head of the coffin. Chairs had been arranged against the walls. All kinds of peo-ple came and went. The mayor and his wife. The local chief of police, Barattucci, and several of the carabinieri. Franca's parents, Marcello and Silvana. Harry French. My old school friend, Luca. Pasquale. My father's cousin, Cesare, who lived in Vasto. Pierpaolo, who ran the bar in the piazza. Even Giacomo, the owner of the seafood restaurant in San Salvo. Towards seven o'clock, the village priest, Don Angelo, appeared and led us all in prayer. Every now and then, my mother would grip the edge of the coffin and peer down into it, as if she was on a ship's deck and looking over the railing at the sea below, and then she would say something, though not to anybody in particular. *At least he's at peace now. At least he can rest.* And then, once again, in a voice that was much shakier, *What am I going to do?*

Getting out of bed, I closed the shutters. As I lay down again, I thought of what Mario had said. *Try to remember the good moments.* What came to me instead was something that had happened long ago. When I was a boy, my father was always taking me out to the plot of land where he grew his fruit and vegetables. One day, he bent over, and when he straightened up he was holding a red bell pepper. Look at this pepper, Gino, he said. This is a female. You know how I can tell? He took the pepper by the stalk and showed me the other end. Three points, you see? A male pepper would have four. His face was alive with the mystery of what he had just imparted, but I couldn't see why it mattered. Male pepper, female pepper—what difference did it make? They all taste the same, I said, don't they? He gave an odd little laugh. They all taste the same, he said, and he smiled and looked down at the earth, which was the source of all his knowledge and wonder, the root of everything he loved. They all taste the same, he said again, and then he lifted his eyes, and his expression wasn't condescending, or even gently mocking. No, it was kind, and that was almost worse, and I remembered how popular he was, nobody ever had a bad word to say about him, and I knew in that moment, even though I was only six or seven, that I could never live up to his example. Did he have any idea, as we looked at each other, that I resented him for being who he was? I don't think he did. He saw my ignorance as a challenge or an opportunity. I was his only son, and he was going to teach me everything he knew. In time, I would surely feel some of the passion that he felt. And I would carry on the work, when he was gone. I would honor the tradition. He was still holding the red pepper by the stalk when I turned and ran back up the hill towards the house. Don't be like that, Gino, he called after me. Gino! But I kept going, and I don't remember looking round. I stroked Franca's hair, then I rolled onto my side, facing away from her, and closed my eyes.

The good moments. Find the good moments.

The funeral took place the next day, at eleven in the morning. The heat was oppressive, the sky almost white. Even so, more than half the village turned out. The church was as full as it had ever been. Old women fanning themselves, Don Angelo's high forehead gleaming. Those who weren't believers gathered outside, in the piazza. Pasquale and Franca's father, Marcello, were among them, standing in the shade, heads bowed. When I walked down the aisle with my mother leaning on my arm, I passed close to Harry, who was sitting at the end of a pew. He was dressed in a dark suit and a white shirt, and his cheeks were wet with tears.

During the week of the funeral, Franca and I stayed at my parents' house. The feeling was that my mother shouldn't be alone. One night, Franca had to go out to dinner to celebrate her aunt Antonella's birthday. The family were celebrating at a pizzeria in Scerni. I ate in the kitchen with my mother, then we watched a drama on TV. After she had taken herself off to bed, I drove over to Harry's house. It was about half past nine when I arrived. He came to the door in a black shirt and black trousers.

I'm not in mourning, he told me. It's just a coincidence.

I couldn't help but laugh at that.

Am I disturbing you? I said.

He gave me his shrewd, narrow-eyed look. I was upstairs, painting.

Painting?

I do a lot of painting when I'm here. He opened the door wider. You want to come in?

I followed him downstairs, into the kitchen, where he poured me some wine. We sat opposite each other. A moth whirled around the orange lampshade that hung above the table.

Thank you for coming to the house the other night, I said. It meant a lot to my mother—and to me.

He lit a cigarette, then leaned back in his chair. This might sound strange to you, since you're Giancarlo's son, but he was like a kind of father to me, even though he was only about fifteen years older.

I saw how upset you were, in church.

I never imagined anything like this would happen. I thought that he'd be here forever. He stared at the ashtray as he tapped his cigarette against the edge of it, then he gave a grim laugh and shook his head.

What he was saying didn't surprise me—my father was a reference point for all kinds of people, and I was used to claims being made on him—though Harry's attachment seemed deeper, perhaps, and more personal, and the thought came to me from nowhere, but with unexpected force, that he was my father's true son, and that he would shoulder the burden of the grief.

Did things improve between you, he asked, in the last few months?

Seeing how important it was to him, I decided that I would lie, partly because I didn't want him to be more upset than he already was, but also because I needed a story for myself, a story I could live with. Collecting all the good moments that I could remember, I merged them into a single conversation, a conversation that had never taken place, but could have, if circumstances had been different.

One evening, I told him, I stopped at my parents' house and found my father on the sofa at the far end of the kitchen. I sat down next to him. Let out a sigh. He said something like, Long day? Pretty long, I said. What about you? And he said, Fancy a beer? I'd love one, I said. I was about to get up, but he put a hand on my arm and said, I'll get it. You want a glass? I shook my head. He took a beer from the fridge and prized the top off, then he said, Mind if I have a drop? Be my guest, I said. He poured an inch of beer into a glass, then handed me the bottle. I thanked him and drank from it, and it went from there, father and son sitting side by side, at ease with one another, talking about nothing in particular. After all, I was married now. I had a steady job and a house of my own. My wife and I were expecting a baby. I had turned a corner, and I was making a life for myself, and he was proud of me—maybe for the first time ever. Glancing at Harry, I saw that the last few words had wounded him, which meant, of course, that they rang true. For the first time ever, I said, we actually got on, and I shook my head, as if in wonderment. I remember saying sorry for all the things that I had done, I went on. He said he was sorry too. We didn't say much more than that. We didn't need to.

Good, Harry said. I'm glad.

It was the story he had wanted to hear—and who knows, if I kept repeating it, it might become the truth. In time, I might even end up believing it myself.

As always, when I saw Harry, I felt better for having gone.

By August of that year, I was at my mother's house less often, though I still visited at least twice a week, usually on my way home from work.

Seventy-six isn't old, she told me one evening, as we sat in the shade of the pomegranate tree, but we never know when we're going to be called. We have to be ready.

I murmured something noncommittal.

Your father lived a good life, she went on. He wasn't afraid of what comes next. He had no reason to be.

Mother, I said, you know I don't believe in all that.

She gave me one of her smiles. At times, the patience she exhibited with me could seem like a form of collusion, as if secretly, deep down, she knew that I had a point, though she would never admit it. Or perhaps she was merely confident that, sooner or later, I would see the light.

He's at peace, she said. I'm sure of it.

I glimpsed my father in his open casket. His face and hands looked oddly yellow, more like cheese than flesh and blood. *At peace.* Whatever that meant. I wasn't about to disagree with her, though. What right did I have to challenge the beliefs that gave her consolation? What kind of son would I be if I took that away from her?

She reached for my hand. He loved you, Gino.

She must think it needs saying, I thought. She must think I'm in some doubt.

She tightened her grip. He really did.

I know, I said.

But I didn't, not really. If love was the ground where nothing but disenchantment grew, what was the point of it? Wouldn't it have been better if my father had felt something other than love? Simple curiosity, perhaps. Or even just interest. I might have been happy with that.

I know, I said, more gently.

That same week, Franca took up the subject, though from a different angle.

Do you miss him? she asked.

It was early evening, and I was standing by the fridge with a cold beer. Franca lay on the sofa, one hand behind her head, the other cradling her belly. Her legs were stretched out in front of her, and crossed at the ankle. On the floor beside her was a bowl of ice. In her fifth month, she had developed a craving for it. I had become accustomed to the squeak and crunch of the misty cubes between her teeth.

In a strange way, I said, I have the feeling that he's still around.

She asked me what I meant.

When he died, I said, he had a poor opinion of me, and nothing can alter that.

You mean, you can't change the way he thinks about you?

Exactly. Because he's gone. I took my beer over to the window. It feels—I don't know—spiteful.

Her laugh was soft, incredulous. You can't call someone dying "spiteful."

Can't you?

The lights of Dogliola flickered on a ridge to the east, as if the village was one big electrical device, and the wiring was faulty. Tufillo, which lay to the south, was hidden behind the trees. The night was heavy with presences and fragrances that my father would have recognized. I knew only a few of them. The wild mustard, whose thick, creased leaves resembled the back of an old man's neck. The bristly, almost barbed stalks of the borage, its flowers the hurt blue of the sky at dusk. The figs in their pale-green skins, each with a teaspoon of sweet brown fruit inside.

It's as if, wherever he is now, I went on, he still has the same idea about me—and that's how it will remain, for all time.

It's not how I see you, Franca said.

Turning from the window, I settled on the floor beside her. I know, and I'm grateful for that. But I can't seem to get away from him, even though he's not here anymore. Somehow him not being here makes him more present than he was before.

You know, he probably wouldn't have changed his mind about you, she said, no matter how long he lived.

I thought about that, but said nothing.

She shifted on the sofa. There's another way of looking at it. Now that he's dead, maybe his view of you can die as well. I mean, who's going to keep it alive? She reached for a cube of ice. If you don't, nobody will.

This viewpoint wouldn't have occurred to me, and I was about to thank her when she let out an exclamation and jerked upright, into a sitting position. The ice cube flew from her hand and skidded across the floor.

It's all right, she said. It's just him kicking.

I put my hand where hers had been and felt a feathery fluttering beneath the tight drum of her skin. A recent prenatal checkup had confirmed that our baby was a boy. We were nearing the end of the second trimester, the doctor had told us, and her only concern was the size of Franca's pelvic canal. You may be looking at a C-section, she said. Franca's response was typically matter-of-fact. *Whatever it takes.*

You want to know what I miss? I said. His fruit and vegetables. The other day, I actually had to buy tomatoes—from a shop.

Laughing, Franca pushed me away. You're terrible.


One Sunday evening, while Franca was with her mother, planning the latter stages of her pregnancy, I called on Harry again. Sitting at his kitchen table, I took the room in properly for the first time. Behind the glass panes in the dresser were several porcelain vases, some decorated with blue-and-white designs, others with Chinese figures in traditional dress. They would be souvenirs of his Hong Kong years. Above the fireplace he had hung two Italian film posters—*The Conformist* and *La Dolce Vita*. On the mantelpiece below, along with a number of smooth, round stones that he had found on the beaches of Abruzzo, was a black-and-white photograph of a blonde woman in a striped skirt. She was relaxing on a harbor wall, the masts of yachts bristling behind her. This was Harry's wife, Rachel. A boy of about eight stood beside her, with one hand on her shoulder, and a dark-haired girl who was younger sprawled on her lap. Rachel had come to Caracciolo with Harry once or twice, but I had never seen the children. They would be grown up by now, I thought. In their thirties.

Don't you ever get lonely, I asked him, being in this house all by yourself?

Lonely? he said. Never.

He gave me a level look, as if challenging me to find what he was saying abnormal or extreme.

Though I was nodding, I wasn't entirely convinced. Why did he almost always come to Abruzzo by himself? Why didn't he bring his family? In an attempt to learn more about him, I asked if I could see his paintings.

His look sharpened. They're not really for public consumption. I do them for myself.

All the same. I'd like to see them.

He sighed, then heaved himself out of his chair and moved towards the stairs.

Bring the wine, he said.

As I followed him to the top of the house, he told me that he had taken up painting when he retired. It was a way of occupying himself. Hours passed without him having any sense of time.

On the top floor, the stairs rose directly into a small room that Harry used as a studio. Double doors led into the bedroom, but they were firmly closed. Another set of double doors opened onto a balcony that had a view of the valley. He had hung several paintings on the walls, but many more were just lying around.

At first, I copied famous works of art, he said.

He showed me a painting of blue flowers that was called *Blossoms in the Night*. Paul Klee, he said. There was another of a man and a woman wearing pale hoods. They were kissing. That's *The Lovers*, he said. Magritte.

In the last year, he went on, I've started trying to paint my dreams.

On his easel was an unfinished canvas. A strip of burnt-orange floated above spiky areas of brown. Below the brown was a white rectangle.

I dreamed I was in Mexico, he said, visiting a white house in the desert. There were mountains in the background. Bare rock—nothing green at all. The sun had gone down, but it wasn't dark. I had done something to upset a local man. I don't know what. He was at the far end of the veranda, consulting with some other men. When he turned and looked at me, I was expecting him to produce a weapon—a knife, perhaps, or even a pistol. But all he did was stand and stare at me. And then I realized. He didn't need a weapon. He could kill me just by looking.

Great dream, I said. But how would you paint something like that?

I'm not sure I can, he said. I'm probably not good enough.

I poured some more wine into our glasses, then I told him about the dream I'd had on my wedding night. Dusk in a service station, the gang in their leather jackets. Pierozzi using a pump to spray our car with petrol. The girl being dragged through the window by her hair. And me with no idea what to do. Me paralyzed.

Pierozzi, Harry said. Isn't he the person things keep happening to?

That's what Silvana says. I hesitated. Also, he went out with Franca before I did.

Harry laughed, but it was out of shock, I thought, rather than amusement. He what?

He had an affair with Franca. It wasn't for very long.

But he's a friend of Marcello's, isn't he? Does Marcello know?

He must never know, Harry. No one must know.

All right. He ran a hand over his bald head. It's none of my business, anyway.

Later, as I drove to Franca's parents' apartment to pick her up, I wasn't sure if I should have told Harry about what had happened between her and Pierozzi. But perhaps I had wanted to unburden myself. It seemed important that somebody should know. And who better than Harry? If he couldn't be trusted, no one could.

Throughout that autumn, I dropped Franca at her office in the morning and collected her at the end of the working day. More often than not, she was to be found in Toni's bar, with an *analcolico* or a glass of ice.

Once, in late October, Michele was leaving the bar as I arrived.

Your wife's inside, he said, then he gave me a toothy grin and moved on up the street.

In those few seconds, he exuded a confidence that I found suspicious. He had referred to something that didn't need referring to, when "good evening" would have done just as well. He had been familiar, even though I didn't know him. But Franca was all smiles when I walked up to her, and I decided to make nothing of it.

Later, though, as I cooked dinner, I realized what it was that I objected to. He had behaved as if he had information that I didn't have. He had made me feel as if I was in the dark about my own wife. *Your wife's inside.* Of course she was. I knew that. I didn't need some stranger telling me.

After dinner, when we were sitting by the fire, I mentioned that I had passed Michele that evening.

Michele? She didn't appear to know who I was talking about.

He was leaving as I arrived, I said. He's tall, with a long neck, and when he smiles you can see all his teeth.

She grinned. Oh him. What about him?

What's he like, as a person?

I don't know, she said. He's harmless. But she had noticed something in me, a curiosity that felt disproportionate or loaded. Why are you interested in him?

I'm not. It's just that he's always there.

He lives round the corner. He has more reason to be there than I do.

I reached for the poker and pushed at a burning log.

There was nothing in what Franca had said that didn't sound perfectly ordinary and innocent, but I couldn't help remembering the way she had talked about Pierozzi once. *He's weak.* When I met Pierozzi, he had seemed anything but weak. It wasn't that I didn't believe her. It was just that I couldn't square her descriptions or responses with my own private observations, and the discrepancy between the two, like the shadowy gap between two tall buildings, was an uneasy place, where all kinds of scenarios might be played out. As always, though, I let the matter drop.

One night in December, I was woken by a noise that came from outside. I switched on the light. Franca's side of the bed was empty. I checked my watch. Twenty past six.

When I called her name, there was no answer.

I had an image of her downstairs, chewing on an ice cube in the dark.

The noise had sounded like a door slamming. It wasn't windy, though. I opened the window and looked out. A blurry half-moon tilted in the western sky, its light low-voltage, silvery. Cold air pressed against my face like metal.

Franca was standing below, on the level ground outside the garage. She was wearing the yellow flannel nightie that her mother had given her, though it looked white in the moonlight. Her feet were bare.

Franca? I said. What are you doing?

My waters broke, she said.

What?

The baby wasn't due until the end of the month.

It's nothing to worry about, she said. Go back to sleep.

I looked at her bare feet. You've got no shoes on. Where are your shoes?

They got soaked. The amniotic fluid.

I'll get you another pair.

By the time I came downstairs with shoes, socks, and a blanket, she was in the kitchen, clutching her nightie around her, shivering. I wrapped her in the blanket, then lit a fire in the grate. Once the sticks caught, I put a log on top, then I made her a cup of hot milk and added a spoonful of Alessio's honey.

She sat on the sofa, holding the cup in both her hands, her eyes on the flames.

Thank you, she said. You're very kind.

She was treating me like a stranger who had found her in distress and had taken her in. The prospect of giving birth had removed her to a new place, far from me.

I asked about her contractions.

Every half an hour, she said. We don't need to bother the hospital just yet.

Leaving her by the fire, I stood on the flat land outside the house. The grass was crisp with frost, and the spindly, almost tortured branches of the fig trees stood out against a sky that was clear and cold and blue. So, I thought. He's coming. And then I thought, Imagine being born today. I had flickers in the pit of my stomach, as if I was about to be tested.

We left for the hospital at half past eight. It crossed my mind, as I glanced in the rearview mirror, that we would never be alone together in the house again, not until we were old, and I felt a thin blade of regret go through me. I wasn't sure if this was a feeling I should allow myself. I tried to concentrate on practicalities. Once your waters broke, Franca had told me, the baby wasn't cushioned anymore, and as I headed south, along the narrow track, then past the white farmhouse with the huge old oak at the front, I slowed for all the bends and did my best to avoid the cracks and potholes. Once on the Isernia road it was easier, since its surface was smooth, and it pretty much ran dead straight. By now, she was having contractions every six or seven minutes. 8:43. 8:50. 8:56. Eastbound, the road was eerily empty. Then I remembered. It was a Sunday.

As we approached the Vasto flyover, I noticed a bar up ahead. I asked Franca if she'd like anything. It might be some time, I said, before we had another chance to eat.

She wanted a cappuccino and a brioche.

The woman behind the bar wore thick black eyeliner and black leather trousers. The only other person in the place was a man sitting in a booth with a glass of red wine. He was reading the sports paper. A sudden and irresistible feeling of self-importance surged through me, as if what was happening to me was front-page news, as if I was at the very center of the world.

My wife's about to have a baby, I told the woman. She's out there right now, in the car.

Is it your first? said the man in the booth.

I said it was.

Good luck to you, he said.

The woman handed me two brioches in paper napkins and placed the coffees on the counter, then she glanced through the window. My announcement seemed to have dredged something up in her, something that wasn't necessarily easy or happy.

I took Franca's cappuccino and brioche out to the car. After she had finished, I ran back with the empty cup. The contractions were coming every five minutes now. The woman behind the bar was drying a beer glass, her eyes still on the window.

You'd better get a move on, she said, putting the glass on a shelf. You don't want her giving birth on the road.

I drank my coffee down in one, then ate my brioche.

She studied me, her gaze knowing and weary, but not unkind.

It'll be all right, she said.

I thanked her, then I paid and left.


In the hospital, Franca was connected to a monitor, and there, suddenly, was our baby's heart, like tiny galloping hooves, rapid but still far away, as though he would have to cross a great plain to reach us, as though it would require not only stamina but persistence. I wondered if he would have what it takes, and I was proud of him for even trying. The little hooves going flat out, the long journey to the world. My own heart, so much older and slower, ached at the thought of it. There were tears in my eyes, and Franca noticed.

Nothing's even happened yet, she said.

A doctor we had never seen before arrived. She told us that our baby was in the breech position, and that a C-section was the only safe option. We had to sign documents to say that we agreed to the procedure. That done, Franca was asked to remove everything that she was wearing—not just her clothes, but her watch, her necklace, even her wedding ring. All her possessions were handed to me, an action that seemed to signify an end, not a beginning. Once again, I found myself on the edge of tears.

A male nurse wheeled Franca out of the room on a gurney. On the way down in the lift, she looked pale and sickly, like a young girl on her first day at school. I held her hand and murmured the obvious things. *It'll be fine. I'm here. I love you very much.* But I didn't like her being taken from me. I didn't like entrusting her to strangers.

On the ground floor, we approached a set of automatic silver doors. I was told that I could go no further. At first, I sat in the waiting room, then I stepped out into a small garden with palm trees, two benches, and a statue of Padre Pio. His face was lowered, mournful—almost tragic. Someone had tucked bright flowers into the gap between his right arm and his chest, and a rosary dangled from his little finger. I felt more alone than I had felt in a long time, and I feared for Franca, behind those silver doors.

At five past one, I thought I heard a cry. I moved back inside. A few minutes passed, then the doors slid open, and a see-through incubator appeared, pushed by a short man with a beard.

This is your son, the man said. He's beautiful.

A chalky substance covered the baby's head like a white cap, and his eyes were shut. His hands were up against his face, closed into fists.

The man told me that he would have to be washed, and that I would see him very soon.

I sat with Franca in a ward with five other beds, four of them empty. I held Franca's hand. I could feel all the bones in it. Her face had a congealed quality, and her lips looked bloodless.

The other new mother was older, in her thirties.

When they cut me open, it was the strangest feeling, Franca said, like they were opening a drawer inside me. Opening a drawer, and taking something out.

How are you feeling? I asked. Are you in pain?

It's not like pain exactly. It's more like I've used a part of myself that I've never used before. She looked past me, towards the door. Where is he? Why won't they bring him to me?

I'll go and ask.

Before I could leave the room, a midwife appeared with our baby and placed him carefully in Franca's arms.

I probably shouldn't say this, the midwife murmured, bringing her face close to Franca's, so the other woman couldn't hear, but this is the most beautiful baby that I've seen in a long time. She paused, then said, Maybe ever.

When the bearded man told me that Elio was beautiful, it had sounded like a truism or a formality, something he said to every new father. This felt different. The midwife looked to be in her fifties. Since she had many years of experience—she must have seen hundreds of babies—you wouldn't have expected her to be impressionable. Nonetheless, she seemed utterly transported, almost shaken.

Beautiful, she said again, then she hurried out of the ward.

The world rushed towards me, closed around me, and I was no longer aware of any noise or any other people. There was only him and me—him lying in his mother's arms, quite still, and me bending over, looking down. His head was perfect, with not a single dent or blemish on it. The vernix had been washed off to reveal a dusting of fine black hair. His nose and mouth were regular, clean-cut. His ears too. His skin wasn't red or wrinkled, but smooth and pale, like snow under moonlight. But it was his eyes that stopped the breath in me. Though misty, they were the dark purple color of an aubergine. Remarkable. I put my little finger into one of his hands and felt his fingers tighten round it.

Isn't he something? Franca said.

I sat with them until about nine o'clock that night, and then, when Elio had breastfed successfully and fallen asleep, I told Franca that I had to go. I had arranged to stay with Cesare, my father's cousin. He lived nearby, in the middle of Vasto. We had agreed that it would make sense if I was close to the hospital, in case of emergencies.

When I walked to my car, I was hit by a fierce and wholly unexpected feeling of relief. It was as though I had been under duress or held somewhere against my will, and now, at long last, I had been released. I stood by the car, one hand gripping the top edge of the open door. The smell of the pine trees nearby. The damp December air. I felt like celebrating—not because everything had gone smoothly, or because my wife and son were safe and well. Not even because I had just become a father. No, I felt like celebrating because I had finally succeeded in putting some distance between myself and what had been happening all day.

As I drove to the *centro storico*, I thought about an encounter I'd had an hour earlier, as I was on my way back from the toilets. A woman in a pale-green dressing gown had approached me in the corridor and said, Are you the father of that baby? She had shoulder-length red hair, and there was a flat place at the back of her head, where she must have slept on it. Which baby do you mean? I said. You know which baby, she said. Her eyes were bright and glittery, and she was clutching at my sleeve. He's extraordinary. Everybody's talking about it. I managed to detach myself from her, though I could feel her gaze on my back as I moved away.

I hadn't said anything to Franca.

I parked in a side street next to Cesare's building. I had last seen him at my father's funeral in June. He had grown up on a farm near Pollutri, but he had been the clever one in the family, the only one to go to university. These days, he wore English-style tweed jackets and small round spectacles with steel frames, and he wrote for newspapers and literary and political journals.

After he had welcomed me into his apartment, he poured me a glass of prosecco. He had been saving the bottle for the right occasion. Also, he had taken the liberty of reserving a table at his local trattoria.

Unless you're not hungry, that is, he said.

I told him I was starving. I'd hardly eaten anything all day.

It's an obvious question, perhaps, he said, when we were seated in the corner of the restaurant, but how does it feel?

So far as I knew, Cesare had no children, and had no interest in children. I had never heard him mention a wife, or even a partner. If he was gay, no one spoke of it. When he offered me a place to stay for a few nights while Franca was in the hospital, it had surprised me, since I wouldn't have expected the birth of my child to have registered with him.

It's hard to say, I said. I've been through so much since I woke up this morning.

Cesare straightened his fork, then reached for a breadstick.

Most recently, I said, I felt relief.

Relief that it went according to plan?

He believed that he was on well-documented ground, and that he already had all the answers to his questions. I felt the sudden urge to shock him out of his complacency, which I could achieve, I realized, by being honest.

Relief to be out of that place, I said. Relief to be away from them.

Behind Cesare's spectacles, his eyes had tightened.

Being there, I went on, it was like being taken through all these different states of mind, one after the other, and every one of them intense. Fear, elation, curiosity, fascination, love, disbelief. There was no letup. I paused. I expected it to be simpler. I paused again. What I expected, I suppose, was joy.

Cesare was listening intently, his breadstick lying on the tablecloth, forgotten.

Once I was outside, I said, the bombardment stopped. There was space around me. I could breathe.

It's your first day, he said. I'm sure it will get easier.

I couldn't help smiling. Even Cesare, it seemed, was capable of platitudes.

Our main courses arrived.

You mentioned disbelief, he said. Why that?

I glimpsed the red-haired woman in the corridor. She had been in a daze, or even in a state of ecstasy. The midwife too.

It's our son, I said. He's beautiful.

Cesare smiled. Once again, he appeared to be making assumptions. What I was saying was predictable—a cliché, really. All parents think their newborn child is beautiful. I needed to choose my words more carefully. Make myself clear.

I'm not speaking as a proud father, Cesare, I said, or even as a new father. I'm being objective. My glass was empty. I filled it from the carafe. His eyes, his nose, his mouth, his hair, his skin—there's nothing about him that isn't utterly exquisite. It's unbelievable. It's almost shocking.

Cesare sat back, dabbing his lips with his napkin. Obviously, I must come and see this exceptional child of yours.

His use of the word "exceptional" told me that he was unconvinced. He would have to see Elio with his own eyes. It was the journalist in him, perhaps.

Just then, I became aware of someone standing behind me. Thinking it was the waiter, I glanced over my shoulder. Enzo Pierozzi was looking down at me.

I thought it was you, he said.

He had two men with him, one in a fawn leather jacket, the other wearing denim. They seemed surprised that he was bothering me, but only mildly. Men like that, I thought, they've seen everything. They don't get fazed. Somebody could be disemboweled right in front of them, and the expression on their faces would be no different.

Pierozzi signaled that they should wait outside. They turned slowly, as if they were sorry to leave. As if they felt they might be missing all the fun. The door opened, then closed. I had to remind myself that the person standing in front of me was the real Pierozzi, not the Pierozzi from the ballroom in Nemi or the Pierozzi from my dream.

I asked him what he wanted.

Are you still seeing her? he said. I'm curious.

His voice was so soft that I thought he could probably do commercials. Luxury soap—or toilet paper.

There's something I want you to remember. Bending a little, he spoke into my left ear. I was there first. There's no getting round that. He glanced towards the door, then back at me. I'll always be there.

In the past, I said. Irrelevant. Forgotten.

But not by you. He smiled unpleasantly, his white teeth showing.

He had been drinking, I realized, but so had I. Words came more easily than usual.

You think I care what you think? I said. I'm the one who's with her, not you.

He straightened up and wiped one hand against the other, as if I was on them somehow, like a residue. Are you sure about that? he said, and then he moved away, towards the door.

I watched through the window as he joined his cronies. He said something to them, and they looked at me, then all three laughed and walked off down the street.

I turned to Cesare. His eyes were calm but wary.

Sorry you had to listen to that, I said.

He dabbed his mouth with his napkin again. Who was he?

Nobody.

He seemed to know Franca.

You can't believe a word he says. He's full of shit.

All right. Folding his napkin, Cesare put it on the table. One thing, though. I don't want him in my apartment.

I shook my head at the idea. That's not going to happen.

Cesare eyed me steadily for a few moments, aware that he was only in possession of a small part of the story, then he looked away.

When the bill came, he insisted on paying.

It's a special day, he said.

It was after midnight by the time I went to bed, but I couldn't sleep. I was in a room that overlooked the road, and even though it was a Sunday night in December, cars kept rushing past, and dense yellow light from the streetlamps pushed through the shutters. I missed the darkness and quiet of the countryside. Also, I was tired to the very middle of my bones. I kept revisiting the moment when Pierozzi appeared at my shoulder. *I'll always be there.* How long had he been watching me without me knowing? Had he been in the restaurant the whole time? I couldn't say, as I'd had my back to the room. One thing was clear, though. If I hadn't got under his skin, he would never have stopped to speak to me. He wouldn't even have recognized me. Perhaps there was some small satisfaction to be found in that.

The next morning, I was making coffee when Cesare stepped into the kitchen, wearing a camel-colored overcoat. He had to go to Milan, he told me. He would be back on Wednesday night. As he handed me a spare set of keys, he gave me a meaningful look.

It's all right, Cesare, I said. It'll just be me.

By nine o'clock I was back in the hospital. I knew that Franca had a large family, but I was unprepared for the number of visitors we had that day. The men stood at the far end of the ward, talking among themselves, or else they stepped out onto the balcony, where they could smoke. The women gathered round the bed, taking turns to hold the new baby or offering advice. No one who saw him failed to comment on his physical appearance, even my mother, who arrived in the late afternoon.

Most babies are ugly, wrinkly little things, she said, but not this one. She looked at Elio. Like everybody else, she couldn't keep her eyes off him for very long. Not this one, she said again, then she put her face close to his and spoke to him directly. You're a bit of a miracle, aren't you.

I was surprised that my mother, who was so God-fearing, would say such a thing, and the word hung on in my head, fizzing and popping, like a faulty neon sign in a dark alley.

When the time came for her to leave, I walked her to her car, and as we emerged onto the road outside the hospital I took her back to that moment.

You said Elio was a miracle.

Every baby's a miracle, she said. This one even more so, because he's yours. She brought her car keys out of her bag, then glanced around her, worried suddenly. The sun had already set, and she didn't like driving at night. Do you know something, Gino? she said. I never thought I'd be a grandmother. Her face blurred into a smile, and she put a cold hand on my cheek. You've given me something to live for.

That's not what I'm talking about, I said. I'm talking about something else. I looked past the parked cars, towards a row of pine trees. They took a step towards me, all at once. I rubbed my eyes.

Are you okay, love? I heard my mother say.

Yesterday evening, I said, only hours after he was born, a woman came up to me outside the toilets. She was actually trembling with excitement. Your baby's beautiful. Everybody says so. That's what she told me—a complete stranger. Doesn't that seem odd to you?

Before my mother could answer, I went on. If I asked you why you used the word "miracle," it wasn't because I was looking for a compliment, or because I wanted you to reassure me. It's just that I keep thinking how strange it is—how *unexpected* it is—that he's so beauti-ful. Because me and Franca—well, we're not like that. I paused, then I said it again. We're not like that.

My mother's features were drawn tight with the strain of trying to understand what I was saying. In that moment, she seemed to find me bewildering, al-most frightening. It occurred to me that perhaps she had never understood me. She had done her duty by me. She had stood up for me. She had loved me uncon-ditionally, no matter what. But I remained a mystery to her. She was still staring at me, still struggling to grasp my meaning, but she couldn't, and that failure hurt her, and made her doubt herself, and that was how I saw her, as we faced each other on the road outside the hospital, as someone who was out of her depth, and wounded.

Looks aren't everything, she said.

You've got it the wrong way round. My hands were up in front of my face, palms open to the sky. I felt a terrible desire to pick her up and shake her. Why couldn't she hear what I was saying? It's as if he's nothing to do with us, I went on. As if we're both impostors. Or perhaps he's the impostor. I don't know.

She was looking up at me, wide-eyed. Be grateful, dear, she said at last. You've been blessed. Once again, she glanced around her, her dry hair stirring in the breeze. Others aren't so lucky.

Okay, I said. Okay.

I opened the car door for her and helped her into the car.

When the door was closed, her face turned in my direction. Be grateful, she said again, her words muffled by the glass.

Drive carefully, I said. I love you.

I watched the car move slowly down the road, its brake lights glowing on and off, though there was no reason to be braking.

After she had gone, I stood in her parking space, not yet ready to go back up. Beyond the pines a green cross glowed. A chemist was still open. Two teenage boys sped past on skateboards. The scrape and trundle of their wheels on the tarmac. A waft of marijuana. I shivered, then turned and walked towards the entrance to the hospital, its glass doors sliding open as I approached.

That night, in Cesare's bathroom, I stood at the sink and stared at myself. Fixed to the top edge of the mirror was a fluorescent tube. The fierce white light allowed for the most detailed scrutiny. I was looking for my son's face in my own, and I could find no trace of it.

It wasn't there.

Be grateful, I murmured. Just be grateful.

I ran the cold tap, then cupped both hands beneath it and brought the water up to my face. I did that three or four times until my mind was empty.

I reached for a towel.

Outside, a motorbike raced past, the noise of its engine as loud and sudden as a gunshot.

Franca was discharged on the Friday, eight days before Christmas. In Vasto, the sun was shining. As we drove inland, however, clouds swirled ahead of us, like water on the point of boiling, and the canes at the edge of the Isernia road bent in the wind. The day before, my mother had asked if we would like to stay with her—at least, to start with. There was plenty of room, she said, and she would be on hand to help, if we were struggling, or simply tired. It was generous of her to offer, though I also sensed the outline of a plea. She was lonely, and we would be doing her a favor. Later, when my mother had gone, I asked Franca what she thought.

I'd like to go home, she said. Then we can be alone, just the three of us.

I swallowed. You think we can manage?

What's the matter? Are you scared?

No.

She looked at me steadily. Even in the dim light of the ward, she could see that I was lying.

All right, I said. Yes, I am. A little.

It's okay to be scared, she told me. It's normal. Leaning over, she checked on Elio. He was asleep. Don't worry, she said, reaching for my hand. If we need help, we'll ask for it. It's just that, since the birth, it has been nonstop people, and I could do with a break from that.

The night before, on the maternity ward, Franca's words had sounded reasonable, and also reassuring—we'd had a flood of visitors, not just family and friends, but doctors, nurses, midwives, porters, and even patients, all of them hoping for a glimpse of the baby they had heard about—but now, in cold daylight, I felt a panic rising through me. Though the direct route to our house was to continue along the Isernia road until the exit for Carunchio, I took the long way round, turning off earlier, at Fondovalle Treste. Franca didn't seem to notice. There were the vines, so stark and bare compared to the lush green of summer. There were the olive trees. How I wished we were going to my mother. Instead, I swung left, over the river, and soon we were up on the ridge that led to Palmoli, the wind pushing at the side of the car, the road surface dark and shiny from the rain.

By the time we turned down the lane that led to La Peschiera, the rain had stopped, though the wind was still blowing hard, and the lone fir tree hissed and shook. Parking beyond it, on the rough ground behind the house, I tried to open myself to the spaciousness and wonder that I had experienced when we first visited, some fifteen months before, but I had no sense of it at all. My feeling of dread had stifled it.

Gino, Franca said, can you take him?

I reached into the back for the carrycot. Elio's eyes were open, and his arms and legs were jerking. I carried him across the wet grass to where the other fir trees stood, roaring and swaying in the wind.

This is the world, Elio, I said. This is your home.

His gaze traveled beyond me, and he made small noises—half gurgles, half sighs. How did it feel to see trees and sky for the first time? What was it like to be so new?

In a few months, I said, the sky will be blue, and the air will be warm, and you can lie here on a blanket, in the shade.

The wind swooped down and ruffled his dark hair. His mouth opened in an O-shape, as if he was shocked or laughing.

Franca came and stood beside us.

You're good at this, she said.

I wished I could believe her, but I felt like a fraud. I couldn't forget those moments in front of the mirror in Cesare's bathroom. I had searched my own face for so long that I began not to recognize the person I was staring at. If I carried on like that, I would not only not find my son. I would also lose myself.

Let's go inside, I said.

Christmas came and went. On New Year's Eve there was a heavy fall of snow. We were back in the house again, after a week of family celebrations and festivities. I stood at the kitchen window with Elio. The last night of the year, white flakes whirling out of a low gray sky. His extraordinary violet eyes were open wide, but his limbs were still, and he was making quiet, birdlike sounds that suggested pleasure and astonishment. As with the wind a few days earlier, he paid such close attention that it was hard not to think of the weather as a performance staged especially for him. The snow became a show, a game—a form of entertainment. There was an aspect to his beauty that surpassed the merely physical. It was deeper, less transient. You felt it as tranquility or rapture.

I recalled how Cesare had appeared on Franca's last day in the maternity ward. Sitting beside the bed, he had stared at Elio. He said all the right things, the things you're supposed to say, but his gaze was forensic, as if this was not a hospital visit but a journalistic assignment.

You weren't exaggerating, he told me later, in his apartment, as he tinkered with an *amatriciana* sauce. He has the typically round head of a baby born by Cesarian section, and his features are exquisite, as you mentioned, but there's something else, something more subtle, yet more powerful. He seems to have the ability to transmit a feeling of well-being. Cesare turned to me, wooden spoon in hand. You must have noticed.

I told him about the visitors we'd had, people we had never met and didn't know. I told him about the red-haired woman in the corridor, and also about the midwife.

He was nodding, as if what I was saying made perfect sense. I don't know how to explain it, he said. It's as though being close to him releases endorphins. As though his mere presence is enough to make that happen. If you could bottle that. He laughed. It sounds far-fetched, doesn't it.

I don't know if I should say this, I said, but if I can't say it to you, who can I say it to?

Cesare's eyes glittered behind his spectacles.

I have the most peculiar feeling, I went on. It's as if he has nothing to do with me.

Though Cesare was still watching me carefully, he seemed to have stopped breathing. Had I crossed a line, even for a man who had no interest in children?

But then I saw him discard one response and reach for another.

I'm sure all new fathers feel that way sometimes, he said. Don't think so much. Just try to be there for your wife. He gave his sauce a stir. It'll all work out.

Platitudes again. I must really have unsettled him.

I had probably overstated my sense of disconnection—*he has nothing to do with me*—and yet a seam of truth ran through my words. I had loved my child when he was inside his mother, and still a part of her. I had loved him when he was an unknown quantity, a notion, a symbol of the feelings that Franca and I had for each other. Now that he was out in the world, though, now that he was a person in his own right, my love felt compromised. Now that he could be touched and held and spoken to, the distance between us, paradoxically, had opened up. I was acting out feelings that were supposed to come naturally to me. I was *pretending* to be a father. In reality, I was paralyzed by trepidation and unease. Was Cesare right when he assured me that such feelings were common, and also temporary, that this was something that was experienced by all new fathers? If that was the case, why didn't anybody talk about it?

My trepidation and unease persisted.

One Saturday in January, as we were returning from a walk, a car drew up behind us. We looked round, expecting to see someone we knew. People were always dropping in with gifts for the baby or food they had prepared for us, especially at the weekend. A middle-aged couple got out. The man was about fifty, dressed in a beige raincoat. The woman had short gray hair, and wore glasses with red frames. I didn't recognize either of them. I glanced enquiringly at Franca. She didn't seem to recognize them either. A light drizzle was falling, but it wasn't cold. The air had an uncanny stillness.

Are you lost? I said.

Lost? The man laughed softly, then his eyes drifted to the woman he was with.

We're looking for a baby, the woman said.

I stared at her.

A young couple who live in this area have had a very special child, the woman went on, and we were hoping we might see him. She looked at the man. That's right, isn't it.

The man was nodding. That's the story we heard.

We stopped at a village, the woman said. They gave us directions.

According to what they told us, the man said, this is the house we're looking for.

Is that him? The woman pointed at the pram. Is he in there?

I'm sorry, I said, but I still don't understand. What do you want, exactly?

To see him, the woman said, and maybe touch his hand.

You're not touching him, Franca said.

But we've driven all the way from Campobasso, the man said.

Franca scowled at him. I don't care if you've driven from the moon. We don't know you.

The couple had moved towards the pram, as if drawn by an irresistible force, and they were bending down and peering beneath the hood, into the shadow where our baby was.

I think you should go now, Franca said.

The strangers paid no attention to her. They appeared hypnotized. In a kind of trance.

I spoke to Franca. Take him inside. I'll deal with this.

She pulled the pram backwards, away from the couple, then set off across the rough grass. The couple straightened up and stared after her. For a moment, I thought they might actually follow her into the house.

Please leave, I said.

The woman had taken the man's arm, and she was looking up at him. Everything we heard is true. Her face seemed flushed, almost scalded, as if she had stood too close to a fire.

The man was nodding. It's all true.

Suddenly, I snapped. Get out of here, I shouted. Now.

The man flinched, then lifted both his hands, palms facing me.

Calm down, he said. We're going.

I stood in the drizzle until the sound of their car sank into the silence and stillness of the day.

That evening, after dinner, I went and sat by the fire with Franca. I wanted to know how a couple from Campobasso could have heard about our baby. Campobasso was more than an hour's drive away.

If they've heard of him in Campobasso, I said, they will have heard of him in other places too.

Franca thought I was exaggerating. Even if that's true, they won't necessarily do anything about it.

I'm not so sure. Didn't you see the look in their eyes?

She nodded. They were like fanatics.

I told her what Cesare had said on the last night I spent in his apartment before we came home.

When he saw Elio, I said, it made him feel good.

He said it was like a release of endorphins. I paused. If Cesare felt it, other people are going to feel it as well.

This place is hard to find, Franca said. That's in our favor. A new thought occurred to her. Now she was grinning. And anyway, she went on, he might get uglier as he grows up. He might start looking more like you.

But I wasn't about to be deflected by one of her jokes.

We need to do something, I said.

The following day, I found an old plank in the outhouse and cut it down to size, then I gave it a coat of white paint and left it in the sun to dry. Later, I painted on the wood in big red letters. PRIVATE PROPERTY. STRANGERS NOT WELCOME. At dusk, I nailed my homemade sign to the fir tree that marked the limit of our land. I walked a little way down the road, then I looked back at the house. To the west, above the ridge, the sky was a brooding, burnt-orange color. It was almost dark. Even so, the sign stood out, and was clearly legible. I wondered how much of a deterrent it would be. That couple from Campobasso hadn't listened to a word I said, not until I started shouting.

Towards the end of January, we drove over to Casalbordino to see Agnese. It took her a long time to answer the door. Her legs were worse than ever. Once she was back in her armchair, though, Franca gave her Elio to hold, and the pain appeared to leave her.

He's beautiful, she said, just like people say.

I wanted to know which people.

Anyone who calls on me. Anyone I talk to. Her gaze moved from me to Franca and back again. You must be very happy.

I stepped over to the window. There was the strip of sea that Agnese had spoken of. That day, the horizon seemed too high, as if you would have to swim uphill to reach it. *He's beautiful. You must be happy.* The first phrase leading to the second, as if one was the direct consequence of the other. She meant well, of course. But if I could have been granted a wish, right there and then, as I stood by the window, I know what I would have asked for. A baby who was ordinary.

I looked at him lying in Agnese's arms, alert but peaceful. *Where did you come from?* My disquiet seemed at odds with his serenity, as if I was the new arrival. As if I was the one who had yet to assume a form.

Later, when Franca was in the bathroom, changing Elio's nappy, I asked Agnese about the time she disappeared.

Her face tightened. Who told you about that?

My father, I said.

I liked your father, she said. He was kind to me when others only had cruel things to say. I'm sorry he's gone.

Is it true that you don't remember anything?

It's true. Her eyes glazed over as she thought back. I remember going for a walk. I kept going until I reached the place where the road met another road, then I came to a standstill. It was early evening. Summer. She raised her glass to her lips, her hand trembling a little, and took a sip. That's all.

What do you think happened?

She put down her glass and looked at me. A ripple or shudder seemed to pass through her, and also through the air between us. Her gaze was cold and heavy.

Nothing good, she said.

Franca returned from the bathroom with Elio.

We should go, she said.

By then, I was back at work, but Franca told me that hardly a day went by when a stranger didn't turn up at the house. Sometimes they were locals—from Caracciolo, or from villages nearby. Other times, they came from the far corners of Abruzzo. There were even people who drove up from Campania, Lazio, or Puglia. Very few were put off by the notice that I had nailed to the fir tree. Though outwardly deferential, they were almost without exception bloody-minded and persistent. Nothing could discourage them from knocking on the door and asking to see the child, and if by chance they were afforded even a fleeting glimpse of him they were always loath to leave. The strange thing about Elio was, he had a way with them. He viewed each new person with an affection that felt both genuine and remote, as if he was touched by them but lived at a more rarified level, or in a different world altogether. After they had spent time with him, they seemed to feel, each one of them, that he had seen into their very souls. To be seen, or known. To have the feeling that you've been understood. There's no one on God's earth who isn't going to be affected by that. Once, on the road outside the building where Franca's parents lived, Elio happened to smile for no apparent reason, and the woman who was with us at the time—a neighbor—began to cry with joy. I remembered what Cesare had said. *If you could bottle that.* We could charge people, I realized. We could make a fortune. But it didn't seem like a good thought to have had. In the end, none of it was good—not for him, and not for us.

It was almost a relief when our local priest, Don Angelo, appeared at our house. He came one weekend in February, in the late afternoon, the day unusually warm and bright. Inviting him in, we offered him a glass of wine. He told us that he didn't drink, but he took a seat at the kitchen table.

I've come to see the baby, he said.

With his round eyes and his high forehead, he had a startled look, and I had to remind myself that this was his natural expression.

You too, Father? Franca said.

I have to admit that I'm curious, he said. I've heard so much about him.

He had scarcely finished his sentence when a cry came from the next room. Franca excused herself, returning moments later with Elio in her arms.

As soon as Elio saw Don Angelo, he gave the priest his full attention. Did he somehow realize the significance of Don Angelo's position in the community? Or was it simply that a new person had arrived? He might even have been fascinated by the silver cross that glinted against Don Angelo's black robes. It was impossible to tell. He seemed watchful, but also receptive. As for Don Angelo, he didn't behave as other people did. There was no adoration, no sense of disbelief. Oddly, his expression mirrored Elio's. The priest and the baby regarded each other with a kind of equanimity, as equals might.

You will baptize him, I trust, Don Angelo said at last.

Of course, Father, Franca said. We've been a bit distracted, that's all.

We've had a lot of visitors, I said.

The priest nodded. Members of my congregation have mentioned it. Even the sisters have been talking about it.

They just keep coming, I told him, day after day. We're at our wits' end.

I saw the notice, Don Angelo said. I hoped that it didn't apply to me. There was amusement in his eyes, though the smile didn't quite reach his lips.

You're always welcome, Father, Franca said.

He inclined his head in gratitude.

The notice hasn't made any difference, I told him. They don't pay the slightest attention to it.

Perhaps their need is too great, Don Angelo said. And then he added, more mysteriously still, Perhaps they don't see themselves as strangers.

He told us that the region was characterized by a deep affinity with magic and superstition. The use of badgers' hair, red coral, or the horns of an ox to ward off the *malocchio*, for instance, or the burning of olive branches at Easter to find out if your luck was good or bad. It was conceivable that the phenomenon of an exceptional child could awaken beliefs that had been lying dormant. In that sense, perhaps, the stream of visitors wasn't so surprising.

I glanced at Franca. I hadn't seen it in that light, and I didn't think that she had either.

You might encounter jealousy, Don Angelo said.

Jealousy? I said. Who from?

He looked at me as if the answer should be obvious. People who wish they had a child like yours.

Later, when Franca asked him for advice, he recommended fortitude and patience. I'm sure it will pass, he said, in time. Then a possibility occurred to him. His expression became pensive, and also, I thought, intrigued, and he added, So long as there isn't a miracle, that is.

Once again, I didn't follow.

If a blind woman comes to visit you, for example, he said, and all of a sudden, after being in the presence of your child, she can see.

He gave me his usual startled look. This time it couldn't have been more appropriate.

When he had gone—he had a meeting to attend, he told us—I closed the door and turned to Franca. I was smiling, but it was a strange smile, with a sickly edge to it.

We'd better start praying that a miracle doesn't happen, I said.

Praying for a miracle not to happen, she said. That's a first.

I nodded gloomily. I know.

Two weeks later, on my way home from work, I called in at my parents' house, but my mother wasn't home. I drove on, through the village. As I passed the bar in the main piazza, I caught a glimpse of Pasquale through the steamed-up window. On a whim, I parked and went in for a drink. Pasquale was on his fourth beer. I bought him a fifth. He told me that an old friend, Salvatore, had recently driven up from Naples and cooked for him.

Cod with black olives. Pasquale waved a hand in small circular motions, as though wafting the fragrance of the dish towards him, then he glanced at me quickly, almost furtively. How's the baby?

Fine, I said.

I hear you've been getting visitors. People you don't even know.

I nodded. They come from all over. Mostly at weekends.

What do they want?

I don't know. I took a long pull on my beer. They seem to think they're going to have some kind of spiritual experience.

Tell them to get lost. Pasquale had no time for God, or for the Catholic church. Communism was his religion, if he had one at all.

I tried that. I even made a sign and nailed it to a tree. FUCK OFF AND LEAVE US ALONE. It's no good. They just keep coming.

Pasquale grinned. Did it really say that?

What?

The sign.

I shook my head. Our house is becoming a shrine, though. If we're not careful, it'll be like living with St. Anthony or Padre Pio. I paused. It'll be like Lourdes.

Pasquale was still grinning. You want another beer?

A few minutes later, the door of the bar swung open and Luca walked in. He had Giotto with him, and also the mechanic who had repaired my father's car.

Look who it is, Luca said.

I hadn't seen Luca and Giotto in ages, not since the night we spent at Giotto's great-aunt's house in the valley.

Luca, I said, how are things?

He nodded. Pretty good. He exchanged a subtle look with Giotto and the mechanic. How's married life?

I couldn't be happier.

Apparently your baby's gorgeous.

How would you know? You haven't bothered visiting.

Babies, he said. Not really my thing. He turned to Pierpaolo, behind the bar. Three vodkas. Large. He faced me again. No offence, but how did someone like you manage to have a good-looking baby?

Pasquale stepped in. Give it a rest, Luca.

Luca pushed one hand through his long, straggling hair, then he reached for his vodka and drank. I'm just saying. I don't get it.

There's nothing to get. I pushed my chair back hard, its legs screeching on the floor. Haven't you got anything better to think about? Is your life that fucking empty?

Luca was smiling, but his smile was blighted, like chrome sprinkled with rust.

You want to get high, Dopey? Giotto said.

I don't do that anymore. I finished my beer, then stood up and put a hand on Pasquale's shoulder. Nice to see you.

Outside again, I hurried across the road to my car. Sitting behind the wheel, I could see the bar, its window a square of grimy yellow in the dark. His shoulders hunched, his head jutting forwards, Pasquale was on his feet and gesturing at Luca. I thought I could imagine what he was saying. *Why are you being so hard on Gino?* Like most people in the village, Luca respected Pasquale, and appeared to be taking him seriously.

I was fortunate to have Pasquale on my side.

For the next few days, that unpleasant encounter kept resurfacing. I couldn't free myself from it. *Apparently your baby's gorgeous.* It seemed that I'd become a laughing-stock. Franca too. I had always thought of our love as something confidential, ever since our secret assignations at the convent, and moving into La Peschiera had increased that sense of privacy, as it had severed our ties with other people, and even, to some extent, with the village. In saying, I don't get it, Luca had reminded me keenly of my own bewilderment. Because the truth was, I didn't get it either.

I didn't realize that I had become short-tempered and distracted until my boss, Raul, took me aside and asked if the baby was keeping me awake at night. You seem overtired, he said. Perhaps you need some time off. Paternity leave, he added, unable to resist a mocking smile, since he was old school, and didn't believe in such things. No, no, I told him. I'll be fine. But I was aware that I had received a warning. The irony was, work had become a kind of sanctuary for me. None of my colleagues had set eyes on Elio, and news of his effect on people had yet to reach the office.

Luca, though.

It wasn't what he had said so much as what he had chosen to leave out. Thinking back, I detected the lurking shadow of an insinuation, a theory or rumor that he had heard but hadn't dared to voice, not with Pasquale listening. Only when I was driving home one night in early March did I finally realize what he had been implying. Though sickened, I was astonished that it hadn't occurred to me before. What if the baby was someone else's?

What if I wasn't the father?

I took the Fondovalle Treste turning and drove for several minutes, my mind stunned into blankness, then I pulled over to the side of the road and stopped. Switching off the engine, I stared through the windscreen. Dusk was falling, but the clouds to the west had been torn open, and the last of the sun was pushing through the gash, less like light than liquid, an ooze of deep, dark red, the hills and vineyards ominous below. It was quiet. No sound of dogs, or even birds. The air smelled of woodsmoke. There would be a farmhouse close by, hidden in a fold in the land. A fire burning in the hearth. The warmth of home. If the baby wasn't mine, then everything made sense. Not just the fact that he didn't look like me, but the creeping, almost morbid sensation I had had, that he had nothing to do with me. That I was convenient at best. At worst, beside the point. Superfluous. It explained why it had been such a relief to leave the hospital on the day that he was born. It explained why I'd had to invent my feelings, why they hadn't come naturally to me. That detachment, that unease—it all fell into place. Going further back, it even explained Franca's apparent misgivings about her pregnancy, when she first learned of it. *You don't think it has come too soon?*

I looked around.

The wound in the sky had closed. The vines stretched away in their neat rows. A dark ridge beyond, and the lights of a village. The world so still.

If the baby wasn't mine, whose was it?

I stood in the dirt at the edge of the road. In the stillness I thought I heard stifled laughter. My throat ached as if I had been shouting. What could I do? Where would I go? What was to become of me?

Headlights appeared. A truck had turned off the Isernia road and was coming in my direction. When it drew level, there was a clashing of gears and a groan from the brakes. An unshaven, middle-aged man with tousled gray hair looked down at me from the cab.

Need a hand, son?

No, I'm fine, I told him. Everything's fine.

But there had been a catch in my voice when I said "everything," and the truck driver continued to look down at me, through his open window, as if he could only leave once I had succeeded in reassuring him. I was in the absurd position of having to come up with a lie for a complete stranger—a man I would probably never see again—in an attempt to stop him worrying.

I said the first thing I could think of.

I was caught short, I'm afraid. I gestured at the grass verge, as if he might want to verify whether or not I had in fact relieved myself.

Wait till you're my age, he said with a good-natured laugh. Happens all the time.

Then he shifted into gear and drove on.

I don't know what was in my mind as I made my way home that evening. Thoughts came and went, flimsy, incomplete. I kept circling back to the truck driver, perhaps because I couldn't bear to think of anything else, or perhaps because of the concern that he had showed. He had wanted to help, and I felt, as I recalled his patient, lined face, that he was somebody I could have confided in, right there and then, on that lonely country road. *My wife's just had a baby, and I don't think I'm the father.* He would have looked straight ahead, through the windscreen. Ah, he would have said. Or perhaps he would have turned off the engine, climbed down out of the cab, and stood beside me, in the dying light. Perhaps he would have offered me a cigarette. He might even have given me advice—or, if not advice, a few moments of companionship at least. I saw his world as a place of kind words and considerate acts, and if I returned to him it was because he seemed like a lost opportunity. He had stopped when he could so easily have kept going. He had given me the time of day. I could have talked to him, and he would have listened. But I had lied—out of embarrassment and shame. *I'm fine. Everything's fine.* In not telling the truth, I had made sure that our lives stayed separate, distinct. Even then, amazingly, he had managed to reveal something of himself. A vulnerability. And I had let him go.

I could have cried.


At last, I saw the fir tree up ahead, the sign I'd made showing in the dark. STRANGERS NOT WELCOME.

Who was the stranger now?

I parked on the rough ground behind the house. There were lights on in the upstairs corridor, and also in the small window high up in the back wall of the kitchen.

Franca kissed me when I walked in, then moved back to the stove. You're late this evening.

For her, it was a night like any other. She had been alone all day, and she was happy to see me, but I felt only sickness and despair. How long had I stood at the edge of that deserted road? Long enough for the red ooze of the sun to blacken, long enough for darkness to come down. A darkness that I felt might never lift. I was struggling not to say things that I knew would damage us forever. I couldn't even go and look at my son, who was sleeping in the next room. I couldn't look at him for fear of what I might see.

Any visitors? I said.

She smiled. Not today, thank goodness.

I asked if I had time for a shower before dinner.

Of course, she said.

Once upstairs, in the bathroom, I stood at the window. The branches of the overgrown fig tree seemed to mimic the fierce tangle of my thoughts. There was more to find out, much more. Things could only get worse. I remembered what Agnese had said when I asked her what she imagined had happened to her. *Nothing good.* I shook as I undressed. Why had I decided to have a shower? It was as if I was the guilty party. As if I was the one who had a crime or a sin to wash away.

During the days that followed, I carried suspicion in my belly like a hard, cold weight that I couldn't dislodge or dispose of. If Franca noticed, she didn't let on. Perhaps it was in her interest to behave as though everything was the same as always. Or perhaps it had occurred to her that I had guessed the truth, and she was hoping that I would doubt myself. *Franca loves me. Franca would never hurt me.* Over Christmas, at her parents' apartment, she had compared Elio to her grandfather, Muzio Magliani, a man I hadn't met, or even seen a picture of, and I began to wonder whether the whole thing might not be one long game of smoke and mirrors. In deceiving me, she was also attempting to put my mind at rest. If you don't recognize your son, she was saying, it's because he takes after my family, not yours. He's the image of grandpa, isn't he, she had said again, during a Sunday lunch in February, and someone had agreed, someone who remembered the dashing fisherman who had died in a storm when he was only forty-nine. That was the cover story. And if it served Franca's purpose, it also, to some extent, served mine. It was an explanation I could give to friends, should I want to save face. He looks like Franca's grandfather, apparently, I could tell them, and then, if I felt like having a laugh at my own expense, I could add, Thank God.

I kept thinking back, though. Elio's due date had been the end of December, in which case he would probably have been conceived in March of that year. What had happened in March? On weekdays, we'd had our jobs to go to. At the weekends, we were busy with the house. One night, Harry had turned up with a wedding present. He had stayed for dinner. But no, she was already pregnant by then. She had told me the next day. What about earlier in the month? There was the time I was delayed for an hour in the office. I walked into Toni's bar and found Franca drinking with another man. Michele. When I asked Franca about him, she told me that he was a local. He was "harmless." Her dismissive attitude should have reassured me—but it hadn't. Could Michele be the father of my child? Somehow I doubted it. I had an image of him in Toni's bar, at the corner table, hanging on Franca's every word. He was attracted to her, but he hadn't slept with her. If he had, his body language would have been different. He would have been less attentive, more relaxed. And physically speaking, it made no sense. With his long neck and prominent teeth, he looked even less like Elio than I did.

And then the world decided to take a hand in things, as the world sometimes does. It was a minor coincidence, hardly deserving of the name, but the effect on me was profound. One spring evening, as I drove home from work, I decided to call on my mother. Soon it would be a year since my father's death, and though everybody praised her for her courage and her pragmatism, I knew that she was lonely. As always, I followed the road that wound its way through the woods, curve after curve, until it arrived at Caracciolo. I was halfway up, not far from the track that led to the famous oak tree, when a black Range Rover came round the bend towards me. Now that it was April, the evenings were lighter, and I had a clear picture of the driver, even though I only saw him for a second or two. There was no mistaking those striking features, that lustrous head of hair. It was Enzo Pierozzi. Our eyes met, then he was past me. I pulled onto the grass verge and put the handbrake on. Why had I stopped? I didn't know. My heart was thudding, as if I had narrowly avoided an accident. But he had been on his side of the road, and I had been on mine. There had been no possibility of a collision. It was something else.

And then I knew, and the nausea rose through me so fast that I barely had time to throw the car door open. I vomited on the broken tarmac at the edge of the road. In the fraction of a second that Pierozzi's face flashed before me, another face had flashed before me too. The face of Elio, my son. Was Pierozzi the answer to the question that had been plaguing me for weeks? Was he the father of my child?

I closed my eyes, then opened them again.

The sickness had gone, but my mouth tasted sour, and a chill had settled on my skin. It wasn't safe to be parked where I was, on a bend. Local people always drove too fast. Someone could run straight into me. Yet I made no attempt to move. On the day of Elio's birth, in that bar on the outskirts of Vasto, I had felt that I was at the center of everything, but I wasn't. Pierozzi was. It was his baby, not mine. I was at the center of nothing.

I rubbed my face with both hands, as if I could erase the knowledge, but it was still there when I looked through the windscreen again. I felt so stupid. I had showed up at his workplace in the hope of wiping out the past, but it hadn't occurred to me to think about the future. In any case, he wasn't the kind of man who heeded warnings or feared threats. Until I appeared out of the blue like that, it was possible that he had forgotten all about Franca—it had been a fling, yet another woman that he had had, one of many—but I had reminded him of her particular existence. He still felt hurt that she had rejected him, perhaps. It had been revenge, not just on me, but on her too. Equally, he might think that if I had gone to all the trouble of tracking him down there must be something special about her, something he had failed to appreciate. He didn't like the idea that he might have missed out. What was it? He had to know. Then again, he might have seen my decision to confront him as a provocation. He might have made it his business to sleep with Franca one last time, just to spite me, or get even. He knew where to find her. San Salvo, in the middle of the day. I could picture his Range Rover confidently parked on the street outside her office. They would have driven to one of the hotels that she had mentioned. The Sabrina, the Nettuno. The Venezia. Or maybe they pulled into a lay-by on the Adriatica and did it in the car. That would have saved him the price of a room. Yes, it was quite possible that I was to blame with my ill-judged, unnecessary bravado. I had brought the whole thing on myself. But what was Franca's role in it? That was harder to discern—unless she had lied about who ended the affair. Had she been too proud to admit that Pierozzi had dumped her? And when he proposed one final rendezvous, for old times' sake, had she told herself that it was worth the risk, that there was no way I would learn of it? Had she found the prospect irresistible? A flashed kaleidoscope of images. Franca lying naked on a double bed, with Pierozzi crouching over her. The black hair on his arms and wrists. Her belly pale, her thighs parted. His hands exploring—greedily exploring…I lowered my forehead onto the steering wheel. I almost willed a tractor or a truck to hurtle round the bend. I would never know what hit me. When I lifted my head again, it was already dark, and the trees seemed to have closed over my car. What had become of the good fortune I had thought we were blessed with? What had happened to that run of luck?

I don't know how I got through that week, or the one that came after. I suppose the truth is, we have resources that we never knew we had. I kissed Franca every morning, when I left for work, and I kissed her every evening, when I returned. In the office, I did everything that was expected of me. Ironically, Raul took me aside and praised my new energy and focus. At home, I comforted Elio when he was crying. I read him stories to help him go to sleep. I told him that I loved him. Inside, though, I felt numb and hollow, as if I had been vacuum-pumped. All the feelings had been sucked out of me. All the goodness. I couldn't rid myself of Pierozzi. The daylight fading, the Range Rover coming round the bend. His face in the windscreen, half-turned towards me. His hair so black, the whiteness of his teeth. Those two seconds played in my head, over and over.

One Friday night in May, Franca asked if I would look after Elio while she went to a cousin's surprise birthday party in Gissi—unless of course I wanted to come, she said, in which case we would take Elio with us. Since I had no interest in her cousin, who I hardly knew, I told her I would stay at home and babysit. It would be good for her to have a night out for a change, I said.

She kissed me on the lips. That's sweet of you.

It was only after the sound of the engine died away that I realized I was on my own with Elio for the first time. My chest tightened, and my palms were damp. Something was about to go terribly wrong, and if that happened it would be my fault, all my fault, and I would never be forgiven. I wanted to run out of the house and just keep running, the moon bouncing in the sky, the breath jagged in my throat and lungs, like a saw going through a plank. I pictured myself on the Isernia road, on the hard shoulder, dazzled by the headlights of oncoming cars.

Elio was on a blanket on the floor, surrounded by his toys, but he was restless. I picked him up and fed him the bottle that Franca had prepared. When he had finished, I carried him upstairs, put him in his cot, and tucked him in. It was early, not even eight o'clock. He was lying on his back and looking up at me. I switched on his revolving night-light. Colorful shapes began to fly smoothly round the room. Pink and blue and orange.

Would you like a story? I said.

His arms and legs jerked frantically.

I started telling him about his great-aunt Agnese. One summer evening, I said, when she was seventeen, she went out for a walk. She crossed the rough grass behind the house, then turned past the fir tree and set off up the road. The weather was warm, and the world was peaceful. There wasn't any wind at all. Ten minutes later, when she reached the junction, she heard a whirring sound. To her astonishment, a silver spaceship dropped down through the air, landing in the olive grove on the far side of the road. The doors slid open, and several aliens appeared. The aliens were like small, glowing clouds that hovered at head height. They asked Agnese if she would be interested to see their planet. She would be very interested, she said, but she had to be back in time for dinner. They promised that she would. So off they went, to outer space.

I glanced at Elio and saw that he was fast asleep, which came as a relief, as I had no idea how to end the story. Obviously, I couldn't use the part about Agnese losing her memory and being found in a church, wrapped in a sheet. That would be too frightening.

Back in the kitchen, I had a simple supper of cold meat, cheese, and bread, then I sat in front of the TV. I don't remember what I watched. I longed for Franca to come home.

Somehow, an hour passed.

At half past nine, I went upstairs to check on Elio. Pieces of colored light whirled gently round the walls. Everything was quiet. Was he still breathing? Nervously, I peered into his cot. He was lying on his back, as before, and his arms and legs were moving spasmodically again.

What are you doing awake? I said.

All his limbs went still, and he seemed to focus on me, his eyes less misty than usual, and darker, more intense.

Who are you? he said.

Cold sweat on my forehead, I gripped the edge of the cot. How could he be talking? He wasn't even five months old.

You're not my father.

His voice was soft, a softness that was all too familiar, but it was also accusatory, as if I was pretending to be something I was not. I picked up his favorite lime-green rattle and held it out to him. He took it and threw it to one side without even looking.

Where's my father?

I backed out of the room, into the corridor.

The gently whirling bits of pink and blue and orange light seemed like objects hurled in my direction.

Downstairs again, I sat on the kitchen doorstep and lit a cigarette. There was a flurry in my head, like a snow globe that had been shaken hard. A million particles, all tiny, jostling. I blew smoke towards the fig trees and watched it bloom, then fade. He couldn't have spoken. He couldn't have. I'd imagined it. All the same, I didn't dare go back up.

The air shifted, like someone moving his weight from one leg to the other.

I lit a new cigarette from the old one. After smoking half of it, I put it under my heel and trod on it. I studied the gold band of my wedding ring, turning it on my finger, round and round. Slowly, the night settled, and the inside of my head quietened down, all the little particles at rest.

Sometime later I looked up, and Franca was moving towards me, out of the dark. She seemed in a hurry. One of her high heels caught in a tuft of grass, and she almost tripped.

What are you doing down here? she said. Elio's crying.

I looked at her, uncomprehending. What?

Can't you hear him? she said.

I hadn't even heard the car.

She brushed past me, pushing me out of the way. What did you do?

I didn't do anything, I said.

*He was the one who did something, not me.*

But Franca was already running up the stairs.

I found her in the bedroom, holding Elio. She had her back to me, and his face was turned sideways against her neck. His shoulders shook once or twice, but he was no longer making any sound. He didn't look at me. Nor did she. They could have been alone together in the house.

I stayed in the doorway, at a loss.

How could you just go on sitting there, she asked me later when Elio was asleep again, with him crying his eyes out?

I was about to go up, I told her. I was just finishing my cigarette.

Had I even been smoking when she appeared?

It didn't look like that, she said.

What did it look like?

I honestly wanted to know. Because I wasn't sure.

It looked like you were deliberately ignoring him, she said. Like you didn't care.

I pretended to cast my mind back to the moments before she arrived. An impossible task, like trying to remember amnesia.

I was thinking about something, I told her. I was in another world.

She was still staring at me, arms folded.

What could I blame it on?

I think it's all these people turning up, I said. I find myself dreading the sound of a car, the sound of human voices. It's been really difficult.

You don't think it's been difficult for me? she said. I'm here all day.

I reached for her and put an arm around her waist. I looked up into her face. I'm sorry, I said. It won't happen again.

She held my gaze, then I saw her soften. You have to be more responsible.

I promised that I would. I was still looking up into her face. She had a glow about her, as if she had been dancing.

How was the party? I asked.

That night I lay awake while Franca slept.

In my mind, I kept approaching Elio's cot and gripping the rail in both hands. When I looked over the edge, I couldn't help remembering how my mother had peered into my father's coffin. But this wasn't a dead man. This was a baby.

*Who are you?*

A crawling up the back of my neck, into my hair.

I found it chilling that the name that had come to me with almost supernatural force in that ruined temple was a name that Pierozzi might himself have chosen. It was four letters long, like his. It began with an "E" and ended in an "O." Like his.

It was as if, at some deep level, I had known the truth all along, but had been unable to admit it to myself.

On a hot afternoon in May, I left work early and drove to the concrete plant near Ortona, the edges of the country roads crowded with the yellow of broom and mustard and the sultry crimson of *erba sulla*. Arriving at twenty past five, I pulled up just before I reached the gates. I was facing west, into the hazy sunlight. All the windows in the car were open. To my right, through a fence of metal staves, I could see the office. Pierozzi's

Range Rover was parked outside, at a rakish angle to the door. I had no idea what I wanted from him. I had no plan. I simply felt the urge to watch him. To study him. To familiarize myself with his movements, his routines. As I sat in my car, a feeling of purpose or conviction flowed back into me. Though I wasn't actually doing anything at all, I felt more like myself than I had in weeks.

At ten to six, Pierozzi stepped out into the yard. He was wearing a pair of sunglasses and a white shirt with the sleeves rolled back to the elbow. He seemed to have a preference for white shirts. Even at a distance, I could see the dark hair covering his arms. Pausing on the tarmac, he glanced back towards the office. A man I didn't recognize appeared in the doorway. He definitely wasn't one of Pierozzi's sidekicks from the restaurant in Vasto. The two men exchanged a few words, both of them gesturing. I couldn't hear what they were saying. They were out of earshot.

At last, Pierozzi gave the man a wave, then walked to his Range Rover. Seconds later, he was speeding through the gates of the plant, wheels raising dust and grit. He didn't notice my car—or, if he did, it stirred nothing in him. He was too self-involved and self-regarding to be much of an observer. I wasn't afraid of him, or what he might do. I was merely curious— and more about myself than about him. I was interested in what I might be, or what I might become, and following Pierozzi was a way of finding out. He was like a laboratory in which I could determine my true properties.

To my surprise, he drove south on the Adriatica. I had assumed that he would take the *autostrada*. You had to pay, but it was quicker, and he was that kind of man. He didn't have any time to waste, and money was no object. My hope was that he was going home. It was important for me to know where he lived. I wanted knowledge about him that he didn't have about me. Knowledge that he wouldn't expect me to have. *He's weak. Sometimes he couldn't even get it up.*

I recalled something that Franca had said to me on the night we kissed for the first time. She had been talking about the popular boys, the boys she wouldn't have dared to approach. How they had all the advantages, and we had none. How that, paradoxically, gave us power. A power they would never have. I had listened to her carefully and found that it made a kind of sense to me—I *wanted* it to be true, perhaps—but I couldn't have given her an example of it actually happening. Now, though, as I followed her ex-lover in his sixty-thousand-euro top-of-the-range Range Rover, I thought I had a better understanding of how it worked. Why did we have power? Because we had no expectations, great or otherwise. Because we had nothing to lose.

As we approached Fossacesia Marina, the Adriatica running close to the beach, Pierozzi indicated, then pulled off the road onto a wide strip of pavement. Had he realized that I was tailing him? It happens all the time in movies, but as a rule, in ordinary life, people don't get followed. Also, I had taken the precaution of allowing a gap to open up, and there had often been two or three cars between us. As I passed the Range Rover, I saw him get out. A flash of the lights as he pressed LOCK. He wasn't looking in my direction. If I parked on the same pavement, I would be too close, so I swung left onto Via Lungomare, a slip road that ran almost parallel to the Adriatica, and put the car in neutral. I watched Pierozzi in my rearview mirror as he crossed the pavement and entered a run-down pale-yellow villa. Bolted to a wrought-iron balcony on the first floor was a sign that said DÉJÀ VU NIGHT CLUB. Under the name was the silhouette of a voluptuous woman seen in profile. She was on her knees, with her head tilted back. Her tangle of long hair almost touched her heels. I looked at my watch. Ten past six. It was a strange time to be going to a strip club.

I sat back, but kept my eyes on the mirror. Usually, I was home by six thirty at the latest. I wasn't sure if it made sense to wait. What if he was having sex? In the event, I didn't have to worry. Pierozzi reappeared after only a few moments. Glancing in both directions, he crossed the pavement to his car. As he drove past me, I bent sideways, pretending to be looking in the glove compartment, then I shifted into gear and followed him.

Fifteen minutes later, he turned off the Adriatica abruptly, at Via Trave, and accelerated up the hill that led to Vasto. Some distance short of the *centro storico*, he signaled left. Not wanting to lose him, I did the same. We passed the sporting club. One glance in his rear-view mirror, and he would see me. I touched the brake, allowing him to pull ahead. A sign said PRIVATE ROAD, but I kept going. There weren't many houses, and almost all of them were hidden behind high hedges and lush vegetation. The road climbed, then leveled out. As I came round a bend, I saw Pierozzi turn in through an electric gate. Before the gate slid shut, I glimpsed a driveway curving downwards and the peach-colored sidewall of a modern villa. I pulled up beyond the entrance, on the grass verge. I wasn't sure of the address, but I would know how to find the house again. Looking around, I noticed an unpaved track leading off the road, not far from Pierozzi's gate. If I parked on the track, under the trees, I would be able to watch him come and go, and I wouldn't be too obvious or too visible. I had no idea why I might want to do such a thing, or what I might hope to gain by it. Perhaps watching him without him knowing was a form of revenge in itself. He'd had things his own way for far too long.

I drove home that evening feeling happy with the progress I had made, and when Franca asked what had kept me I told her that Lidl was being audited again.

I didn't want to bore her with the details, I said, but there would probably be some more late nights during the next few weeks. What I was saying sounded credible, and since she had never really understood what my job entailed she didn't think to query it.


Every three or four days, after work, I drove straight to Pierozzi's house. I would park on the unpaved track, beneath the trees, his electric gate lined up in my windscreen. I would listen to a jazz CD and smoke a cigarette or two. It was the only time when calmness descended on me. It was like a medication that I had to take in order that the rest of my life could happen. Ironically, perhaps, given where I was, I was able to forget about Elio, and the evening that I had spent alone with him, when he told me that I wasn't his father. Placing myself in close proximity to Pierozzi allowed me to believe that I had gained the upper hand. I began to find things out. His wife drove a Fiat convertible. She was slim, with a blonde ponytail, and she liked to dress in pale colors—oatmeal, nutmeg, cream. She wore a lot of gold. As yet, I didn't know her name. There were children as well. On Tuesdays the son had a tennis lesson. He would appear in an immaculate white T-shirt and white shorts, a racket under his arm. I put his age at eight or nine. The daughter was younger, about six. She was called Clarissa. When the gate slid open, I saw the villa with its wide sun terrace, its terracotta urns, and its freshly watered lawn. Beyond it was the Bay of Vasto and the huge blue sweep of the Adriatic. Clearly, there was a good living to be made in concrete. But as I sat behind the wheel of my ordinary car I wasn't envious. I had the life I wanted. The only aspect of it that troubled me was Pierozzi's role in it. Looking at what he had, though—at least, the little that I saw between six and six thirty in the evening—I couldn't help but feel mystified. In embarking on the affair with Franca, he hadn't merely jeopardized his friendship with her father, Marcello. He had also jeopardized his whole setup—the trophy wife, the luxury property, the perfect children. It surprised me that he would want to take so big a risk—unless, of course, his entire existence was built on risk. Did he always have a woman on the go? Was that why he had called at that tacky nightclub on the Adriatica? I wondered if his wife was in the dark about his infidelities, or if she knew and had decided to turn a blind eye. It might be the price she was prepared to pay for the lifestyle he had given her—or perhaps they had an open marriage, and she had affairs of her own. I couldn't see it, somehow. She didn't seem the type. Even if that was true, though, think how she would feel if she found out that he had a child by another woman. For all my uncertainty and torment, there was a sense in which I was holding all the cards. A winning hand, you might say. But what game was I playing, really?

Perhaps it couldn't have gone on. Perhaps, like a criminal, I was flirting with the idea of being caught. Or perhaps I wanted him to know that I had been watching him. Yes, that was it. I wanted him to know.

On a fine June evening, I had been parked under the trees for about ten minutes when I sensed the Range Rover approaching. Though I had become accustomed to the sound its engine made, my instinct told me that Pierozzi was close before I heard a thing. Like a cat, I could feel it in my marrow. I was that attuned.

As the Range Rover edged into view and the gate slid open, I saw that Pierozzi's wife had left her Fiat in the middle of the drive. There was no way past. Pierozzi had no choice but to reverse back onto the road and park outside his house, on the grass verge. Judging by his expression, this annoyed him. I couldn't help smiling. Petty of me, perhaps, but it always entertained me when small things went against him. As he got out of his car, he happened to look up the track, and his eyes met mine. He hesitated, but only for a second, and then his face hardened. Slamming the door, he strode towards me. I suppose I must have realized that, sooner or later, a confrontation would take place, but I hadn't prepared for it. In that moment, I was more interested in seeing how he was going to react.

I saw this car the other day. I'm sure I did. He put his hands on the roof and looked down at me. What are you doing here?

I'm on my way home from work, I said. I thought I'd stop for a while. Unwind a bit.

You're outside my house.

I gave a shrug. That could be a coincidence.

You expect me to believe that?

There's no law against parking here.

This is a private road, he said. Residents only. Also, you're harassing me and my family.

I took a breath and let it out slowly. You didn't listen to me, did you. You didn't take me seriously.

What are you on about?

You saw her again. You couldn't help yourself. Or maybe you just did it to spite me. People like you probably get off on shit like that. I looked up at him. Take your hands off my car.

You're insane, he said. But he had stepped away. He glanced towards the house, then back at me. I'm calling the police.

Call them. I don't care.

He had his phone in his hand, but he wasn't punching any numbers.

I suddenly remembered Franca's mother talking about him at Sunday lunch. Her words came to me like ammunition.

You're the kind of person things happen to, I said.

His head came up fast, and his eyes had darkened. What's that supposed to mean?

Things happen to you. Things go wrong.

In the background I could hear a woman's voice.

That'll be your wife, I said.

She had appeared at the entrance to their property in a white jersey dress and high-heeled sandals. She looked expensive, but uncertain.

I'll be right with you, Pierozzi called out. Go back inside.

She didn't listen, though. She stayed where she was, on the driveway.

I know where you live. I chuckled. I never thought I'd actually say that to someone.

Get the fuck out of here, he said quietly.

I started the car, not because he had told me to, but because I felt like it. I had said everything I wanted to say, and I had kept all the important details to myself. He had no power in the situation. The fact that he had sworn at me was proof. *He's weak.*

As I turned past the villa, he was talking to his wife, but she was looking at me, as if she was trying to work out who I was. I pointed two fingers at my eyes, then I aimed the fingers at her husband. *I'd watch him if I was you. He's dodgy.* Her head moved back—she must have taken a quick, unexpected breath—then she was in the rearview mirror, getting smaller and smaller, and I was heading down the hill, towards the Adriatica.

One Tuesday evening not long afterwards, Franca's parents invited us for dinner. That lunchtime, Marcello had bought fresh fish, and he had decided to make a *brodetto*. Antonella and her husband, Ciro, had driven over from Lanciano. Pasquale arrived with Harry French and a rucksack containing several chilled bottles of Pecorino. Harry was wearing a white dinner jacket over a black shirt. I didn't know James Bond was coming, Marcello joked. Harry dropped into a 007 pose, with an imaginary gun. As usual at family events, though, it was our son who was the center of attention, with people taking turns to hold him. He hadn't spoken to me again, but I lived in fear of it, and tried to avoid being alone with him. I still had the feeling that I was a stand-in or caretaker. For a six-month-old baby, he was uncannily composed, and I saw his steady gaze as a kind of holding pattern. He was waiting to see what I would do.

The *brodetto* was a great success, and as the plates were cleared away and Antonella brought her home-made apricot tart to the table Elio began to cry. Franca carried him into an adjoining room.

Strange about Enzo, Silvana said suddenly.

She appeared to be looking in my direction, and I wasn't sure why, but what struck me was the timing of the remark. Had she deliberately waited until her daughter couldn't hear her?

Enzo? I pretended not to recognize the name.

Pierozzi, she said. Marcello used to spend a lot of time with him. She paused. Not so much anymore.

No. Marcello grinned for no apparent reason. Not so much.

What about him? Pasquale asked.

Someone put a bomb in his letterbox, Silvana said.

Everybody at the table fell quiet.

It blew up the electric gate, apparently, she went on. Destroyed a section of the wall. She brushed a few breadcrumbs off the tablecloth and into the palm of her hand, then tipped them onto her side plate. One of the villa's windows was shattered by the blast.

Was anybody hurt? Harry asked.

Silvana didn't lift her eyes from the table. Luckily, there was no one home.

He has two young children, Antonella said. Imagine.

Ciro was shaking his head. Who would do a thing like that?

Marcello exchanged a look with Pasquale, which Silvana saw.

What? she said.

Marcello said that one of the reasons why he had been seeing less of Enzo was that he had begun to suspect that Enzo might have Mafia connections.

I glanced at Silvana. She met my gaze, but kept her face expressionless.

He's in construction. Marcello helped himself to a second slice of apricot tart. In a way, it would be surprising if he wasn't mixed up with them.

Everyone was nodding except for Pasquale, who reached for the corkscrew and started opening another bottle of Pecorino. He disapproved of gossip and speculation. He took no part in it. In that respect, and that respect alone, he bore some resemblance to my father.

Franca appeared at the table, and I made room for her. She told me that Elio had fed well. Hopefully, he would sleep for a while.

You think he upset somebody? Ciro was asking.

Basically, it's a warning, Pasquale said. Next time— if there is a next time—it'll be much worse. He was abrupt, almost rude. The subject bored him, and he wanted to put an end to it.

Silvana, who had been quiet since she broke the news, turned her dark eyes on her husband. You remember what I always say? Trouble follows him around.

Marcello nodded, but said nothing.

You should think about not seeing him, Silvana said.

I haven't seen him in months, Marcello said. Not since April.

He was turning his empty wineglass on the table, his mouth tense, the pouches of skin beneath his eyes discolored, swollen. He seemed tired suddenly, or chastened. Perhaps he sensed that his friendship with Pierozzi was being viewed as an error of judgment.

Looking at Silvana, I thought what I often thought. She might not say much, but when she did choose to speak it was always significant. She saw things other people didn't see. Which made it all the more peculiar that she hadn't linked Enzo Pierozzi with her daughter, or with me. I kept quiet, though. I didn't want to seem too interested. After all, as far as the Magliani family was concerned, the man who was being discussed was simply one of Marcello's friends, somebody I had never met.

Later, as Franca drove us home, she asked what we had been talking about while she was breastfeeding Elio. She was sure she had heard the word "Mafia."

We were talking about Pierozzi, I said.

What about him?

Someone put a bomb in his letterbox.

God, is he okay?

Somehow, that seemed like the wrong response. I had been hoping she would be indifferent to the attack, or even, possibly, condone it. *He had it coming. Serves him right.*

He's fine, I said. He wasn't there.

Thank goodness for that.

I almost wish he had been there. It might have shaken him up a bit.

Gino, that's an awful thing to say.

Well, maybe he deserves it. Maybe he's an awful person.

How would you know?

Our headlights poked at the darkness on the road. Corners flung themselves at us. Trees leaned in, and then away.

Are you defending him? I said.

She glanced across at me. How much did you drink this evening?

What's that got to do with anything?

You seem to be trying to pick a fight with me.

I'm not. I'm really not.

We were on our way down into the valley. In five minutes we would be home. I was talking to myself inside my head. *Don't say it. Whatever you do, don't say it.*

Curve after curve, dark trees overhead.

Nothing on the road.

Franca parked at the back of the house, then she was walking away from me, through the rough grass, Elio looking back at me, his head showing above her shoulder, his face impassive.

*Who are you?*

I followed them, but Franca was acting as though I didn't exist, as though it was just her and the baby, returning home. I felt irrelevant, beside the point. If I had not been there, it would have made no difference. I stood on the level ground at the front of the house. Is he okay? she had said. And then, Thank goodness.

You haven't seen him again, have you?

There. It was out.

She was over by the door. Bending awkwardly, she was trying to fit her key into the lock. I should have been helping, since she was also holding the baby.

She looked at me sidelong. Seen who?

Pierozzi.

What do you mean, seen him?

Her voice was cold, and her narrow face seemed to have closed against me. Once again, I told myself to forget it. It wasn't too late. I knew I couldn't, though. I had to know.

Did you ever see him again, I said, after we started going out together?

Why would you ask that? She adjusted the position of the baby in her arms. Don't you remember what I told you, when we were sitting in that alley, on the steps?

I nodded miserably.

I meant it, she said. I've never said that to anyone.

There was still a way back—she was showing it to me—but something in me had become rigid or stubborn. I was destroying everything that I held dear. I couldn't stop myself.

Franca, I said, you still haven't given me an answer.

Her face was suddenly tight with anger. At last, she realized what I was implying.

Fuck you, she said. Fuck you for even asking.

With her free hand, she took the car keys out of her pocket and threw them at me. They struck me on the chest and fell to the ground with a dull clink.

Leave, she said. I don't want you in my house.

Where am I supposed to go?

I don't know. I don't care. Just go.

I stared at her.

I don't want you here, she shouted, her voice so loud that it seemed to bounce off my chest, just as the keys had done.

The baby started crying.

You see what you did? Stroking his head, she started whispering to him. It's all right. Everything's all right.

It's my house too, I said quietly.

Just go, she said.

I picked the keys up off the grass and turned away. As I walked back to the car, a light clicked on in the upstairs corridor, and Franca moved past the window. She didn't look my way, though she must have known that I would be out there, in the dark.

The car keys bit into the palm of my hand.

Out of habit, I headed south, towards the Isernia road, but when I reached the junction where the white farmhouse and the oak tree were, I stopped. Once again, I remembered what had happened a week or two earlier, when Franca was at her cousin's birthday party, and I was alone with Elio. *You're not my father. Where's my father?* The night was still. Moonlight silvered the inside of my brain. I sat behind the wheel and shivered.

Without understanding why, I turned the car around and drove back towards the house. I took one of the bends too fast and plunged into a wild hedgerow. You're drunk, I told myself. You shouldn't be driving. The car's wheels spun in the undergrowth, but I managed to reverse. I carried on, more slowly now. Would Franca hear the car? Would she think I was returning? I saw her bent over the cot, her head angled towards the window. No one else used the track after midnight. As I approached the house, I seemed to be listening with her, the sound of the engine coming closer and closer, and then passing the house, and dying away, the rumble fading to a hum, then nothing.

I considered turning up at Giotto's great-aunt's place. I couldn't bear the thought of running into Luca, though. I'd had enough of his remarks. Imagine how he would gloat when he learned that Franca had been unfaithful. I could always go home, but I didn't want to worry my mother. Since my father's death, she had become a light sleeper. She would hear the car on the drive or the front door opening, and she would appear in her dressing gown, her hair askew, and ask me what was wrong. And I would have to tell her. All the same, I found myself taking the road to Caracciolo. As I passed through the piazza, the church clock struck twelve thirty.

I parked halfway up the hill, next to the chapel, then walked down a flight of steps and stopped outside Harry's house. Lights were still on, and classical music was playing. I knocked on the door that led into the kitchen. I waited a few moments, then knocked again. Looking round, I saw a small girl squatting on the second-floor balcony of the building opposite. She was watching me through the railings.

That's Mariangela.

I swung round. Harry had answered the door without me noticing. He was no longer wearing his tuxedo.

She likes to spy on me, he said. She thinks I'm mad. Mariangela, he called out, why aren't you in bed?

The little girl sprang to her feet and ran inside.

Harry smiled.

I'm glad you're still awake, I said.

I'm listening to Brahms, he said. Third Symphony. Do you know it?

I shook my head.

Well, you should, he said.

I followed him into the kitchen, with its warm, terra-cotta-colored walls and its window that over-looked the valley. He turned the music down, then poured me a glass of wine. We took seats at the table.

Franca threw me out, I said.

What did you do?

We had an argument. I looked at the cigarette that he was smoking. Could I have one of those?

He pushed the packet and the lighter across the table towards me.

I took out a cigarette and lit it. You've seen our baby, right?

I saw him this evening. He's great.

When you look at him, I said, and then you look at me and Franca, what do you think?

Strange question.

Tell me, Harry. Honestly.

He leaned forwards and stubbed out his cigarette. What are you getting at?

I began to talk, and it all flooded out of me. Our child was extraordinary-looking, but we were not. We never had been. Our nicknames at school had been "Dopey" and "The Rat." Our child's beauty was a mystery to me, I told him, and also, more recently, a source of anguish. On the night Harry let me see his paintings, I had told him about Franca's affair with Pierozzi, but now I went further, saying that I feared that she had taken up with him again, and that the baby wasn't mine, but his.

Harry was shaking his head long before I finished.

Franca would never do that, he said.

How can you be sure?

Haven't you noticed the way she looks at you? I saw it when you were twelve or thirteen, and it's still there now.

He poured us both another glass of wine. The Brahms symphony had ended. He put on Brahms's Violin Concerto, another piece of music he thought that I should be familiar with.

You're the only one she cares about, he went on. The only one she's *ever* cared about. God knows why.

I couldn't help grinning.

Didn't she ask you to marry her, he said, when she was nine?

She didn't ask. She told me it was going to happen.

You see? That's Franca. You really think she'd throw all that away?

You haven't met Pierozzi. He's—

Impatient, Harry talked across me. I don't need to meet him. He leaned over the table, eyes glittering in the narrow gap between their lids. Yes, your little boy is beautiful. You know why? He's the beauty inside you that you didn't know about, the beauty that you couldn't see. He paused. If you hadn't had him, you'd probably never have realized.

I stared at him, but couldn't think of a response.

You didn't even know it was there, Harry went on, but he's the evidence. The proof. And if you're doubting it, or scared of it, or trying to destroy it, it's because you're too stupid to see that.

I was still staring at him, but I was thinking of what my mother had said when she was standing outside the hospital on the day after Elio was born. *Be grateful. Others aren't so lucky.*

He reached out and tapped my forehead with his index finger. Did it go through that thick skull of yours?

I said it had.

He yawned. I suppose you need a bed for the night.

If that's all right.

He put me in the room above the kitchen. Under the window was a camp bed. On the other side of the room was a desk and a simple wooden chair. The walls were bare except for a large black-and-white photograph of an old Chinese man smoking a long pipe. Another reminder of Harry's Hong Kong days. From where I lay, I could see the lights of Palmoli. Beyond it, in the valley, was our house. Somehow, I imagined that Franca was still awake, as I was. A moon lounged in the sky to the east, a fortnight shy of being full. This was no time for things to be uprooted or cut short.

In the morning, Harry made me an instant coffee and a slice of toast. English breakfast, he said with a wry smile. People in the village always teased him about his cooking.

He would call Franca, he said. He would let her know that I had stayed with him, and that she didn't need to worry. He would tell her that I'd be back that evening.

You're the best, Harry.

It's a phone call, that's all, he said, but listen. This is important. When you see her, you have to say the right things.

The right things, I said. Okay.

He gave me a stern look. I'm serious. Don't mess this up.

I won't.

After thanking him for his hospitality, I put my cup and plate in the sink and left.

Since my car was facing up the hill, I decided to take a different route to work. I drove west out of Caracciolo and up onto the ridge, freeing myself from the crocodile's jaws. The mountains of the Maiella usually looked ominous, like something you could run up against or founder on, but that morning, with the mist cloaking their lower slopes, they seemed almost ethereal. My spirits lifted, the despair of the previous night discarded, forgotten.

After picking up some focaccia from the bakery on the outskirts of Gissi, I took a steep shortcut past an olive grove, and then another through the pines and fir trees, the quickest route to the valley below. The radio was on. I sang along to a song I had never cared for. I felt light in myself, and impatient for the day to be over. I was full of good intentions and resolve. At lunchtime, I would go to the florist near the cemetery and buy Franca some orange lilies. That evening, I would present her with the flowers, and I would tell her that I was sorry. I don't know what came over me, I would say. I love you, Franca. I always have, and I always will. It might make sense, I thought, to steal one or two of Harry's lines. I've had a kind of revelation, I would tell her. Elio's like the beauty in me that I didn't know was there, the beauty I've spent half my life ignoring or trying to obliterate. It has taken me until now to realize, even though you've been telling me for years. I would look at the floor and smile ruefully. If I've been slow, I would say, I apologize. It's time to break with my old destructive ways of thinking. I need to grow up. After all, I'm almost twenty-eight.

At work that day, there were issues—in-store replenishment was out of alignment with consumer demand, and that had led to more markdowns than usual, and more waste—but it wasn't anything that I couldn't handle, and I must have sorted it out efficiently, otherwise Raul wouldn't have asked me to have lunch with him. At least, that was what I thought. Once in the pizzeria, though. Raul told me that I had been underperforming. Turning up late, leaving early. He was starting to worry. Was I really the right man for the job?

I did well this morning, didn't I? I said. Fresh produce orders are back on track.

I know, I know. He took another greedy bite of pizza. In restaurants, he always seemed voracious, like a man who had gone without food for days. You have talent, he said, no one's denying that, but you're unreliable. Erratic.

I was about to blame fatherhood, which was the obvious excuse—and also, as it happened, the real reason for my shortcomings of late—but as I watched him sink his teeth into yet another slice I decided to use the strategy I had used with Franca's family.

I don't know whether you know this, chief, I said, but I've had my fair share of demons, and I've been fighting to overcome them. Just recently—perhaps even as recently as last night—I feel as if I've turned a corner. I'm different now. I'm going to do much better.

Raul was eyeing me with new interest. I appreciate your honesty, he said. Let's drop the subject for a week or two. See how you do. He took a swift gulp of wine, then mopped his mouth with a paper napkin. By the way, I hear that boy of yours is something special.

In the past, that type of comment had either exasperated me or reduced me to despair. Not anymore. As a result of Harry's intervention, I realized I could live with it. I could even feel pride.

Yes, he is, I said. He really is.

All of a sudden, I was grinning. I had thought of a way of entertaining Raul, of drawing him closer.

Actually, I went on, leaning forwards and lowering my voice, as if I was about to let him in on a secret, some pretty weird things have been happening.

Like what? he said.

I told him about the complete strangers who had been turning up at our house. They had learned about the existence of our son, and they believed that setting eyes on him would amount to a kind of blessing. I said I would give him an example. One Saturday, a coach party had arrived.

A coach party? Raul's mouth dropped open.

Fifty people, I said. Maybe more.

The leader of the group seemed to expect a guided tour, I told him. Where could they get coffee and pastries? Was there, by any chance, a toilet they could use? Without knowing it, we had become a tourist attraction. I took the man over to the sign I had put up. What does that say? I said. He repeated the words. *Private property. Strangers not welcome.* He had the stupid, stuffed look that people have when they're presented with something they don't understand. Politely,

I asked him and his party to leave. He began to remonstrate. They had come all the way from Rome. I told him that I didn't care where they had come from. They could turn around, go back again. But people were already stepping down out of the bus, if only to stretch their legs after the long journey. One woman was on her knees in the grass, praying. A tall, thin man with hunched shoulders was moving slowly towards my wife and son, as if under a spell. I want you to go, I shouted. All of you. I grabbed the tall man by the arm. Get back on the bus, I said. He stared at me, startled. The leader of the group was exchanging muttered words with the people closest to him. No one seemed inclined to leave. In desperation, I looked around. Nearby was a heap of earth left over from the hole I was digging for our new septic tank. I picked up a solid lump and flung it at the leader of the group. Striking him between the shoulder blades, it sent him staggering. There were exclamations of outrage from several of the coach party. The way they looked at me, you'd think I was some sort of criminal or monster. Go away, I shouted. Leave us alone. Once again, the leader began to protest, but the praying woman had scuttled back into the bus, and the tall man was cowering, hands up around his ears. I picked up another clod and hurled it at the bus. The earth exploded against one of the side windows. Cries came from inside. The leader of the group scrambled up the steps, and the door slammed shut behind him. I kept throwing lumps of earth until the bus lurched off down the road.

Raul's eyes were wide, but he was also laughing. I've never heard anything like it. No wonder you've been distracted.

That was a couple of months ago, I told him. More recently, I've been feeling differently about it all.

Raul wanted to know how.

Now, when I think of those people turning up, I said, I find it moving.

Moving? Once again, I'd taken Raul by surprise.

Look around you, I said. People are desperate. In need. They're looking for something that will make them feel better about their lives.

Later, as we left the pizzeria, Raul put an arm around my shoulders. I like you, Gino, he said. You're funny. Not just that, though. You're a thinker too.

We walked a few paces. His arm was still draped affectionately around my shoulders, but his eyes were fixed on some imaginary horizon.

I don't want you to worry, he said. Things are going to work out.

I feel that, I said. I really do.

I was eager to see Franca and Elio, but I stayed at my desk until six o'clock, as if to demonstrate my new commitment. By a quarter past six, though, I was on the Isernia road, a low sun in my eyes, a bunch of orange lilies glowing on the seat beside me. That evening, the traffic was chaotic. Near the Montenero exit, a petrol tanker overtook me, engine howling. I glimpsed the driver high up in the cab, silver mirror shades, jaw muscles flexing as he chewed a wad of gum. I repeated what Raul had said on our way back to the office. *Things are going to work out.* He had been talking about my job, but I felt that if I kept saying the words, they might spread sideways until they encompassed every aspect of my life. Since I wouldn't be calling on my mother, I sped past the Fondovalle Treste turning. I was already later than usual, and it was quicker to take the next exit, five minutes further on.

As I turned off the Isernia road, the sun dropped behind the ridge ahead of me. In that warm, gray half-light, I had the feeling that I might hallucinate. At the fork in the road I bore left, as always, following the sign to Carunchio. I drove through a wooded area, and then the trees retreated into the distance and the land opened out, like an ancient battlefield, the ground surprisingly flat and green. Checking my rearview mirror, I saw there was a car behind me suddenly, and that its headlights were flashing. People who were in a hurry didn't bother with their lights. They simply roared past, as the petrol tanker had done. Was it the carabinieri, then?

I pulled onto the grass verge, and a black Range Rover surged past, then parked in front of me, at an angle. *A black Range Rover.* That was the car that

Pierozzi drove. Doors opened on both sides, and Pierozzi got out. The two men with him were the men I had seen on the night Cesare took me out to eat in Vasto.

I stood next to my car.

A bomb. Pierozzi's smile was grim and disbelieving, and his hands were spread in front of him, like someone feeling for rain. Really?

The other men came forwards steadily.

A bomb, Pierozzi said again.

His face seemed to convulse, as if an electric current had passed through it, and all trace of a smile, grim or otherwise, was gone.

I had just realized what he was talking about, and I began to laugh at the absurdity of it. You think that was me?

You dare to try and hurt my family? he said. Who do you think you are?

Before I could reply, something hurtled towards me from the left side of my vision, and my head cracked open. A sharp-edged burst of light, then darkness. I was on the ground. Tarmac. Yellow weeds. Far-off trees stacked horizontally.

Someone was hitting me or kicking me. I wanted to say stop, but I couldn't move my mouth. There was a noise, like a swarm of bees. One of the men walked past, something dangling from his hand. The sound of a window shattering. Little bits of glass danced in the dirt. Someone was still kicking me, and when I tried to explain that this was all a ridiculous mistake he drove a fist into my face and I remember nothing after that.

Opening my eyes was difficult, my eyelids stiff as rusty metal. My head felt numb, but also painful. Slowly, my blurred vision cleared. Franca was sitting beside the bed.

Gino, you're in hospital, she said.

When she bent over me, I could smell her hair. The oils in it, the fragrance. It was too rich. I thought I might be sick.

Don't try to talk. You broke your jaw. She put a hand on my forearm. A farmer found you. You were lying at the edge of the road, unconscious.

Your car's a wreck.

I drifted away, then I came back. I had the feeling that I had left the room, though I knew I couldn't have.

What happened, Gino? She looked down into her lap. Sorry, don't try to talk.

The fist that came from nowhere. A searing flash of light, the yellow weeds. If people get hit in a movie, they're back on their feet in seconds, and none the worse for wear. In real life, it's not like that.

I wanted to move my mouth. It wouldn't move.

I closed my eyes.

When I opened my eyes again, Franca's clothes were different. Flowers stood in a vase next to the bed. The bright colors hurt my eyes. I wondered what had happened to the orange lilies.

It was my father's ambulance that brought you in, Franca said. He looked so worried.

Like the old joke. *See you—or maybe it's better if I don't.*

It's not just your jaw, she said. Your cheekbone's fractured too, and one of your eye sockets, and you've got some broken ribs. Luckily, there was no internal bleeding. She squeezed my hand. You're going to be fine. You'll have a scar, though. Here. She touched the skin below her eye.

Her outfit changed again, and then again.

My mother appeared. So did Marcello and Silvana, Pasquale, and Harry French.

While recovering, I came to a decision. I wouldn't tell anyone about Pierozzi and his thugs. I would pretend not to remember. When Franca asked who had done this to me, I wrote on a piece of paper. *I've no idea.* One moment I was turning off the Isernia road at the exit for Carunchio. The next, I was lying in a bed in hospital. I wouldn't bother Pierozzi again, and I didn't think that he would bother me either. In some strange way that didn't quite make sense, I had the feeling we were even. But I did want to tell Franca the things that I had been planning to tell her on my way home.

About three weeks after the attack, I took her hand.

That fight we had, I said.

She was shaking her head before I could get the words out. Forget it.

I stayed at Harry's house that night.

I know. He told me.

We listened to Brahms. The next day, I bought those lilies that you like. The orange ones.

They were in your car, she said. They had glass all over them.

Someone must have smashed my windscreen.

They looked kind of beautiful like that. She smiled to herself.

I wanted to tell you how sorry I was, I said, and that nothing like that would ever happen again, but I never had the chance. I said some awful things. I don't know what I was thinking.

Nor do I.

I was in a weird state. I think I was under a lot of pressure. I started having doubts—about everything.

She looked at me, but didn't speak.

I should never have doubted you, I said. Please forgive me. I love you, and I love Elio. You'll never know how much.

You're an idiot.

I know.

By the middle of August I had made a full recovery, though I suffered with headaches from time to time, and my jaw clicked when I ate. I still hadn't told anyone about my experience on that lonely country road. I hadn't even told Franca. It would have raised too many questions. The attack on me remained a mystery. I turned off the Isernia road at the Carunchio exit, and I woke up in hospital in Vasto. For me, those were memories that dovetailed, the one fitting neatly against the other. When people asked me what I thought had happened in between, I would tell them that I had no theories. It was all a blank. Or sometimes, when they asked me what I thought had happened I would use Agnese's words. *Nothing good.* As always, given my reputation in the village, there were those who believed that I had brought it on myself. Somehow, I was to blame. Most people were sympathetic, though.

I might have had one or two lingering side effects—apart from the headaches and the clicking jaw, I also had the scar that Franca had predicted, a small L-shape under my left eye—but I felt much better in my mind. The beating I had received seemed to have purged me, drawing all the pain and poison out. I no longer agonized about whether or not I was Elio's father. If I ever found myself having doubts, I would repeat Harry's words, like a kind of mantra. *He's the beauty in me that I didn't realize was there.* I was more grateful to Harry than he knew. I thought of him as my English father—or as the father that I had never had. A whole new generation had been inserted into my family, one there shouldn't have been room for, but one I wouldn't have been without, and every now and then, when I was passing through Caracciolo, I would call on him with little offerings. I enjoyed that smile of his, amused yet puzzled, as I appeared at his door with a book on Cimabue or a bag of ripe figs from our tree. It was thanks to Harry that Elio no longer spoke to me in voices that weren't his. He never had, of course. I had imagined it all. In any case, Elio was beginning to talk in his own voice. Though he wasn't even nine months old, he was already using language, not just obvious words like "mamma" and "papa," but "nose," and "apple," and also—eerie, this—"lily." He was still extraordinary to look at, though slightly less extraordinary than he had been at the beginning, his eyes more blue or gray than aubergine, his hair not quite so sleek and black. Perhaps we were simply getting used to him. Among local people, he had a certain reputation. Like the six-hundred-year-old oak tree, though, he was just another feature of the village that they could be proud of, or boast about. To my great relief, strangers had stopped arriving at our house. I no longer dreaded a knock on the door or the sound of a car's engine on the road outside. I had even taken down the sign.

It was at around that time, coincidentally, that I ran into Don Angelo. I had been helping Pasquale to clean the steel vats in his *cantina*, and as I opened his garden gate and stepped out onto the street I found the priest standing in front of the grocery store, checking his change. He was on his way to see the sisters, he told me, but he was curious to have news of Elio.

He's doing very well, I said.

I'm glad to hear it. Don Angelo slid the coins into a pocket in his dark robes. And how's it going with the visitors?

You were right, Father. Things have settled down.

There have been no miracles? He gave me a smile that seemed playful, as if, in the end, the whole thing had been a kind of game.

If there had, I said, you would have heard.

He nodded. Perhaps the miracle is that he is no different to the rest of us. That's something to be thankful for.

And I am, Father, I said. I'm truly thankful.

He wished me a good evening, then he set off down the narrow street, towards the sisters' house.

One Sunday not long afterwards, I drove to the sea with Franca and Elio. The heat was fierce, and once we joined the Adriatica the traffic slowed to a crawl. A portly Sikh in a mauve turban strolled between the cars, handing out discount vouchers for the circus. I parked in a modern piazza, not far from Giacomo's restaurant, where I took Franca for our first date, then we walked past the holiday apartments to the sea. The beachfront restaurants and ice cream parlors were blaring upbeat music, and there were rows of parasols and loungers on the sand. People were playing volleyball, or standing in the shallows, talking. Late August in San Salvo Marina.

As often happened when we were out with Elio, somebody we didn't know approached us. That afternoon, it was a deeply tanned, elderly woman in a scarlet bikini and heavy gold earrings. She stared at Elio with the rapt or dumbstruck expression that Franca and I had become accustomed to. When she was able to find words, she said all the usual things—such a beautiful child, what a treasure, I don't think I've ever seen, etc., etc.

Noticing an accent, I asked where she was from.

Calabria, she said. I'm here on holiday.

Have you been to Abruzzo before?

She shook her head, sun glancing off her earrings. It's my first time.

There's something you should know, I said. Our son's really nothing special. He's just a typical Abruzzese child.

Even through her sunglasses, I could tell that her puzzlement and disbelief were tempered by the desire to learn a new, astounding fact.

They're all as beautiful as him?

I nodded. The beauty of the children in this region. It's our best-kept secret.

I had no idea, she said. She was already looking around to see if there were any other babies in the vicinity.

I wished her a happy holiday, then I put my arm round Franca's waist and we moved on, along the promenade.

Franca nudged me in the ribs with her elbow. She believed you, the poor woman.

Well, it's better than being rude, I said.

Later, on a dusty plot of land set back from the beach, we came across the fairground that was a fixture in San Salvo every summer. Once in among the attractions, I searched for the merry-go-round, and there it was, the animals surging past me on their upright silver poles, the music jangly, unhinged.

Remember the tiger I hit on the Isernia road? I said to Franca, pointing at the animals. It was just like one of those.

Elio was pointing too, delighted by all the colors and the noise.

That day I had three rides in a row, with Elio in front of me, clutching the pole, and Franca looking on, arms folded, smiling, and I felt I had attended to something that should have been attended to much earlier.

Whatever had been out of kilter had been adjusted, and now, at long last, it was on the true.

In early September, on my way home from work, I called in to see my mother. The air was humid, dense. Gray clouds edged in pale orange hung above the village. There would be a storm later on.

My mother was sitting at the side of the house, in the shade of the pomegranate tree. Franca's mother, Silvana, was with her. The two women were sharing a bottle of cold beer. I fetched a glass from the kitchen and sat with them, aware of Silvana's eyes on me, watchful and dark.

It's been more than a year, my mother said, but I still can't believe he's gone.

He was a good man, Gabrì, Silvana said.

My mother nodded slowly, then she sighed. I know. I was lucky.

Did he really foil a fascist plot all by himself? I asked.

No, my mother said with a chuckle. He just happened to be working for *Paese Sera*, the newspaper that broke the story. He was a junior reporter.

Still, Silvana said. Exciting times.

My mother was nodding again. Tremendously exciting.

I reached for my glass and drank. It came as a relief to hear that my father wasn't the hero that I had been led to believe he was. Now that the part he had played in exposing the fascists turned out to be relatively insignificant, I found that I liked him more. I looked up into the branches of the pomegranate tree. The fruits were close to being ripe. I remembered how he would cut open their leathery skins and free the small red jewels. He had always had such a great desire to teach me things, but I hadn't wanted to learn. Or perhaps the things that I wanted to learn were things that he wasn't capable of teaching. If he had lived longer, that might have changed.

I wish he could have met Elio, I said.

My mother murmured in agreement. He would have made a wonderful grandfather.

Perhaps Elio would have appreciated and absorbed my father's knowledge, I thought. Perhaps that receptive quality had skipped a generation, as looks sometimes do, and Elio had inherited the desire to plant things and to watch them grow. Perhaps Elio would organize his life according to the phases of the moon.

How is that little boy? my mother asked.

He's well, I said.

Bring him round soon.

I said I would.

We lapsed into silence.

A sparrow hawk slid through the hot, still air, the black stripes on its tail clearly visible. In the valley below, the dogs were barking.

Silvana turned lazily to me. Did you hear about Enzo?

Enzo? I shook my head.

His wife caught him with another woman.

Enzo, my mother said. Wasn't he a friend of Marcello's?

Used to be. Lowering her eyes, Silvana adjusted the thin belt on her dress. She's leaving him, apparently. Taking the children. She sipped her beer. Somehow he kept the villa, though.

I never had much time for him, my mother said.

I looked at her, surprised. It wasn't like my mother to pass judgment on others. That was the Lord's work.

Silvana tilted her glass. The last of the beer slid to one side and formed a small golden triangle that caught the light.

Someone really ought to take him down a peg or two, she said.

Driving home that evening, I thought about what I had been told. *She's leaving him.* It seemed like something I had been waiting for, though without knowing it. At the same time, it seemed remote, and of no consequence, like news from a distant galaxy.

I didn't think I'd mention it to Franca.

In February of the following year, Raul asked if I would be up for an early evening drink. He had some issues with the department that he wanted to discuss. Usually, I liked to hurry home after work, but since

it was Raul who was asking, and he had been so sup-
portive during my convalescence, allowing me all the
time I needed, I didn't feel I could say no.

As we approached a bar in the center of Vasto, a car
came along the narrow street towards us. We stood
back against the wall to let it past, but the car stopped
as it drew level, and the window slid down, revealing
the driver. It was a face that I had almost succeeded in
erasing from my mind.

Pierozzi.

Nice scar, he said. How are things?

I'm fine, I said.

How's the wife? How's Franca?

I leaned down and looked past Pierozzi, into the
car. One of the men who had assaulted me was in the
passenger seat. He had the same expression as Pierozzi.
Gloating, and mildly contemptuous.

I straightened up again. In an attempt to respect my
privacy, Raul had stepped a little further down the
street, and he was peering into the window of a shop
that sold men's clothing.

Such a whore, that girl, Pierozzi said. She'd go
with anyone. He turned to his passenger. Have you
had her yet?

If the man replied, I didn't hear it. I was looking
across the roof of the car to the building opposite. An
iron ring hung from the rough stone wall. Long ago,
it would have been used for tethering mules or horses.

Lighting a cigarette, Pierozzi blew smoke at me. Who knows, I might have another crack at her myself.

The man in the passenger seat said something in response, and Pierozzi laughed, then he gave me another mocking look and drove away.

I stood staring after him. He had exchanged his black Range Rover for a black Jaguar.

Who was that? Raul asked.

He had turned from the shop window. Like me, he was staring after the car. I wasn't sure how much he had heard.

Nobody, I said. But I was shaking with anger.

Are you all right, Gino? Raul said. You look a bit pale.

*Such a whore, that girl.*

There she was again, in the Nettuno or the Sabrina. There she was, stark naked, with his hands all over her—

I feel like I'm coming down with something, I muttered. I think I'd better get on home. I managed a quick, apologetic smile. I'm sorry, boss.

Don't worry, he said, and gripped my arm. We'll do it another time.


After that, I started watching Pierozzi's house again. It wasn't deliberate, or planned. I simply found myself drawn back to that private road halfway between the old city and the sea. Like Pierozzi, I had a different car—a car he didn't know, and wouldn't recognize. Nevertheless, I played it safe by parking near the sports ground and continuing on foot. I found a place in among a clump of oleander bushes where I could keep an eye on the house with no chance of being seen. I told myself that I was checking to find out whether or not the story Silvana had told me about Pierozzi was true. I didn't ask myself why I should care, or what I would do with the information. Perhaps I thought, as Silvana did, that someone should take him down a peg or two. Perhaps I thought that "someone" should be me. But more than that, I no longer had the feeling I'd had while lying in my bed in hospital, that we were even. He seemed intent on causing grief and torment, or doing actual harm. At the very least, he wasn't about to let the matter drop.

I soon discovered that the gossip was either inaccurate or out of date. One evening towards the end of March, a glass door slid open at the back of the house, and Pierozzi's wife stepped out onto the terrace. She reached up with both hands, gathering her blonde hair into a ponytail, then she stood at the railing, gazing out over the bay. She looked pensive, but not unhappy. After a few moments, Pierozzi joined her on the terrace. She might have left him in the autumn, as Silvana had claimed, but since then, clearly, there had been a reconciliation. It was possible that she had forgiven him for his indiscretions. Equally, he might have per-suaded her that to carry on living with him was where her best interests lay. Or perhaps they had agreed to stay together for the sake of the children.

I didn't know what I was waiting for until it happened. A few days after Easter, a taxi stopped outside the house, and Pierozzi's wife wheeled a suitcase up the driveway and onto the road. The children followed, each with their own small case. Were they moving out again? Somehow, it didn't look like it. Pierozzi's wife seemed relaxed and calm in her long cream cardigan and her biscuit-colored dress, and the little girl—Clarissa—was chattering cheerfully to her brother. There wasn't a hint of tension or distress.

As I watched, Pierozzi appeared on the drive in a white shirt and sunglasses. He stood by the gate, smiling and waving, as the taxi pulled away. I decided that his wife and children were going on holiday. They were visiting family, or else they were flying somewhere. After all, school had finished the week before. My heart began to beat high up in my throat. So far as I was concerned, their absence meant one thing, and one thing only. Pierozzi was on his own in the house.

The next morning, I called Franca from work. I had a dinner in Termoli, I told her, and she shouldn't wait up for me. I wouldn't be home until late.

When I drove up to the villa that night, the lights were still on, even though it was after eleven. Thinking that Pierozzi was unlikely to go out again, especially as it was a weekday, I chose to stay in my car, which I parked in the shadow of the trees. I smoked a cigarette and listened to a jazz CD on low volume. Charlie Parker played "Now's the Time." Thelonius Monk played "Don't Blame Me." As when you're in love, there wasn't a track that didn't seem appropriate and relevant. The world would be better off without Enzo Pierozzi. I was convinced of that. In the short term, his family might be upset, but in the fullness of time, once they were rid of his conceit, his violence, and his endless deceptions, once they experienced the lightness that his disappearance left behind, they would feel much happier. I was convinced of that as well. I watched him pass a window with his mobile phone pressed to his ear. I hoped he was talking to his wife, and not to some new girlfriend. It would amount to a goodbye of sorts.

By midnight, there was only one lit window left, high up on the second floor. At 12:17 the light clicked off. I decided to wait a little longer. A man walking a dog passed by. Otherwise the road was quiet.

When the house had been in darkness for half an hour, I lifted a fuel can from the boot of the car, then I climbed over the fence and approached the property through the olive trees that surrounded it on the south side. I wore nondescript black clothing and a baseball cap pulled down low over my eyes. Did Pierozzi have a dog? Surely, if he did, I would have noticed it by now. I stood against the back wall of the villa. The Bay of Vasto stretched away below. The long, uncertain curve of lights along the shore, the blackness of the sea beyond. It was an expensive view, even at night. There was an absence in my head, no nerves at all.

I unscrewed the cap on the canister and circled the villa, splashing petrol. As I came round the front, I triggered a security light. I didn't think Pierozzi would notice—he would be asleep by now—and even if he did, he would assume it was a pine marten or a stray cat. All the same, I worked faster, emptying the last of the petrol against the solid wood of the front door. I put the fuel can down and struck a match. There was a big, soft noise as the petrol caught, and I took a few steps back, onto the grass. I had imagined that I would leave the scene immediately, before I was spotted, but the flames had me hypnotized.

Just then, there was a crash and a splintering, and something pale and agitated burst from an upstairs window. It was Pierozzi, trying to escape the fire. He landed on the lawn with a dull thud, not far from where I stood. I found myself laughing. It was all so sudden, and so odd. One of his legs was bent beneath him. Glass glittered in his black hair.

You made me jump, I said, hurling yourself out of the window like that.

I squatted beside him. His eyes were closed, but his lips were moving. He didn't seem to be unconscious.

I was aware of the coolness of the grass.

You've ruined your pajamas, I said.

His face twisted, and he coughed a few words into the ground. Call an ambulance.

I knew they'd be white, I said. You like white, don't you—which makes no sense, actually, because there's nothing innocent about you.

Ambulance, he murmured.

Behind me, in the villa, something huge collapsed. I could feel the heat against my back.

You're lucky to be alive, I said, you know that? You were two floors up!

His eyes opened. Fire flickered across the pupils.

Call a fucking ambulance.

You call it, I said.

Then I rose to my feet and walked away.

As I drove south, along the Adriatica, I had no sense of failure or regret. I was too busy replaying the vision of a man in white pajamas jumping from the upstairs window of a burning house—how he soared, like some frantic angel, past the bright lick of the flames. I was still marveling at the strangeness of it all.

Then blue lights started in my rearview mirror.

# III.
# HARRY

AS ALWAYS, WHEN I returned to Caracciolo, Pasquale invited me to lunch. At one o'clock, I rang his bell, and the gate clicked open. *Permesso*, I called out. *Avanti*, I heard him call back from somewhere inside. I walked through his garden, then parted a bead curtain and entered his apartment. I found him in the kitchen, washing clams. With his curly hair, his firm jaw, and his pock-marked skin, Pasquale wouldn't have looked out of place in a Mafia movie. On our first meeting, I instantly pictured him in a car with Robert De Niro and Joe Pesci, on his way to whack a guy. In reality, he had worked for a heating systems company for thirty years. Like me, Pasquale was retired. He spent his days walking his dog, Nada, and making wine.

That afternoon, he served two courses—*spaghetti alle vongole*, which he knew I loved, and a sea bass that he had bought in Gissi and roasted with potatoes in the oven. When we had eaten the fish, he put a peach on my plate, then he opened another bottle of his own two-year-old Pecorino and set about rolling himself a cigarette. My gaze drifted to the window, which he had flung wide open. Several clouds hung in the bright blue sky, their soft, blurred edges caused by strong winds at high altitude. The Appenines stretched away below, ridge after ridge of wooded land, home to bears and wild boar and even wolves. If you kept going, you would find yourself, eventually, in Rome.

It's so good to be back, I said.

How long has it been?

Almost a year.

Did you hear about Gino? Pasquale's eyes seemed to track down his arm to his hand as he tapped some ash into a cheap tin ashtray.

What about him?

He's in Torre Sinello. He's serving a seven-year sentence.

My stomach turned over. What did he do?

He set fire to Enzo Pierozzi's villa, Pasquale said. Pierozzi was inside it at the time.

I reached for my wine and drank. The previous summer, when Gino turned up at my house at midnight after an argument with Franca, he had seemed obsessed with Enzo Pierozzi. I had tried to talk some sense into him. Obviously, I'd failed.

Pasquale didn't know all the details, only that Pierozzi had escaped by leaping from a window. He was in a wheelchair now. Apparently, he was thinking of selling his concrete business and moving back up north. He was from Brescia, originally.

I asked how Franca was.

I don't know, Pasquale said. I haven't seen her. He drew on his roll-up. It's a real mess.

During my time in the village, I had heard all manner of stories about Gino. He had been expelled from school, he had crashed his motorbike, he had fought with his parents, he had overdosed. Local people always said that he would come to no good. For some reason, though, I had taken an interest in him, perhaps out of loyalty to his father, Giancarlo, who had been a friend since the beginning, but more probably because his waywardness didn't feel entirely unfamiliar to me. Not that we were all that close. When I bought my house in 1988, Gino was only a boy—he would have been nine or ten—and months would go by without us even catching a glimpse of each other, but later, every once in a while, he would seek me out, sometimes when things were going well for him, but more often than not when they were going badly.

When I suggested to Pasquale that I might pay Gino a visit, he told me that it wasn't quite that simple. I couldn't just turn up at the prison gates. I would need the proper authorization.

The following morning, I presented myself at the *comune* and asked if I could see Barattucci, the chief of police. I was shown into an office that overlooked the main piazza. Mauro Barattucci rose from behind his desk and shook my hand. He had a lean upper body and muscular legs, an unusual physique that made me wonder if he had been a cyclist in his youth.

Welcome back, Harry, he said. What can I do for you?

I told him of my desire to visit Gino.

He gave a despairing shake of the head. That young man—what was he thinking?

I would have to apply to the prison authorities, he told me, who would, in turn, seek authorization from a magistrate. Since I was a *terza persona*, my request would also have to be approved by Gino himself.

*Terza persona?* I said.

It's the legal term for someone who isn't a member of the family. Barattucci's eyebrows lifted. You may not be aware of this, Harry, but many of those who have been incarcerated have no wish to be visited by people they know.

That same day, in the evening, I walked over to Gabriella's house. She came to the door, a small woman dressed in black, with brittle, copper-colored hair. We embraced without speaking, then sat down at one end of her kitchen table. She asked after my wife, Rachel. Outside, it grew dark, but she didn't think of turning on the light. Behind her glasses, her eyes were dim and cloudy.

First Giancarlo, now Gino, she kept saying, as if she had lost Gino for good. As if Gino, too, was dead.

Her hand trembled as she poured my beer.

I repeated what Barattucci had said, that I would need Gino's approval if I was to pay him a visit. She promised to mention it the next time she went to the prison. She was sure that Gino would be receptive. I was one of his favorite people, she told me—though her voice was so doom-laden that it sounded less like a compliment than an affliction or a curse.

Towards the end of my second week in the village, I received a document that was covered with official-looking signatures and stamps. The accompanying letter stated that I should present myself at the *Casa di Lavoro* in Vasto the following Thursday, at ten o'clock in the morning.

It's a beautiful drive to the prison. From my house near the top of Via Roma, you head uphill, past the sports ground and the cemetery, then along the crest of a high ridge. To the west, a mountain range known as the Maiella is visible on clear days, and also in the winter, when its peaks and slopes are white with snow. To the north, and far below, beyond the plowed fields and the thickets of oak and broom, the sea shows as a vivid strip of blue. After circling Gissi, its houses clinging to a rocky outcrop, you drop down into a valley, then follow a road that is wide as a racetrack, and lined with tall stands of marsh cane and extravagant clusters of pink and scarlet oleander. Once you have passed through a small *zona industriale*—a sheet metal works, a textile business, a restaurant—the land is occupied by vineyards, and the wineries they serve. Finally, you reach the old two-lane main road that runs almost the entire length of the coast, from Ancona to Bari. Drive south for a few minutes, and the prison appears on your left, the plain, sand-colored blocks built on a low bluff that overlooks the Adriatic. People like to joke that the convicts have sea views.

Arriving at the gatehouse, I handed my passport and my authorization papers to a woman with a weathered face and tired blonde hair. Though she was friendly enough, there was a hushed or somber undercurrent to our exchange, almost as if I was entering a place of worship. After storing my belongings in a locker, I was escorted down a tunnel, then across the no-man's-land that lay between the perimeter wall and the prison itself, up a flight of concrete steps, and into a bleak, scoured room, where I was subjected to a thorough search. You wouldn't believe some of the things that people try to smuggle in, the guard told me with an easy grin. I didn't think to ask what kind of things. The sense of being in a sacred space persisted. I felt oddly nervous.

Once admitted to the Visitors' Room, I took a seat at a plastic table. Fans revolved lazily on the ceiling, but the air was soupy, thick. The woman at the next table wore her dyed black hair in a high ponytail, and her dress was divided vertically, one half leopard-print, the other half black. When our eyes met, she frowned, then studied her long nails.

At last, a green metal door opened, and Gino appeared. I stood up and gave him a hug. He smelled clean but chemical, like cheap deodorant.

Dear Harry, he said. I knew that you of all people would come to visit me.

He sat down at the table. His face looked thinner than I remembered, and he'd had his hair cut short, but he was smiling—a reluctant, slightly mournful smile that reminded me of his father. The last time I had seen him was in the hospital, after he had been found unconscious on a road near Carunchio. Fifteen months had passed since then.

You're a good friend, Harry. One elbow on the table, he passed a hand over his cropped hair. I'm sorry you have to see me like this.

You've lost weight, I said.

Have I? Maybe I have. The food's terrible—though not as terrible as the stuff you cook. He gave me a grin. The old Gino, for a moment. The Gino who had christened me "The Frenchman."

How long have you been in here?

Three months. He looked off into the room, but nothing seemed to register. It feels longer.

I would have come before, I told him. I only just got back, though.

You've been in Wales, with your wife?

Yes.

How is she? How's the family? Everything good?

Gino, I said, what happened?

He looked at me again, his eyes so wide and concerned that, for a second or two, I felt I was the one who was in trouble.

I tried to kill Pierozzi, he said.

I know, I said. Pasquale told me. But why? I thought that story was over.

He took a breath and let it out slowly. I thought so too. But it wasn't.

A man at a neighboring table tore open a packet of biscotti. The sudden, vicious crackle of plastic made Gino flinch.

Do you remember the first time we met? he said.

With your father, you mean, when I bought my house?

I didn't really speak to you, not then.

Halloween, I said. I dressed up as a vampire.

He grinned. I don't know what we were expecting, but it certainly wasn't that.

You were one of the kids that kept coming to the door. You kept saying you weren't scared.

Did I?

I nodded. You were a bit annoying, actually.

His grin widened. You were good to me, though. You've always been good to me. If you saw me, you'd say hello and ask me how I was. He passed a hand over his head again. You've always been here for me, Harry—not like those other bastards.

The people in the village, he meant.

You never judged me, he went on, even if you thought I'd been an idiot.

Ah well, I said. We've all been idiots.

I'm not sure my father would agree. He pushed back the sleeves of his gray hoodie and scratched absentmindedly. His left forearm was fretted with small red cuts, all roughly parallel.

I looked away from him, across the room. On the wall were murals that featured a cottage with a thatched roof, a waterfall, an urn of sunflowers, a streetlamp, and a pair of swans. Apart from the sunflowers, the rustic scenes seemed distinctly un-Italian, and though I understood that they must be intended to lift the spirits, the mixture of crude nostalgia and fantasy had the opposite effect on me.

There's a silver lining to all this, Gino said. At least he's not around to see it. Not that he'd be surprised, probably. But still, I couldn't bear to have him at this table, with that long-suffering face of his.

I felt the need to stand up for Giancarlo. I'm sure he loved you, in his own way.

In his own way. Gino let out a bitter laugh. That just about says it all, don't you think?

When our time was up, he asked me to visit again, but his voice was tentative, as if he was worried that I might turn him down. I told him I would put in a request for the following Thursday. I could come every week if he liked, I said—while I was in Italy, that is.

Thank you, Harry, he said. I appreciate it.

Only as I crossed the flat, featureless area that separated the prison blocks from the high wall that surrounded them did I realize that he hadn't mentioned Franca or his son, not even once.


That evening, after dinner, I called Rachel. As always, she told me about her day. In the morning, she had pruned the roses that grew against the back wall of the house. The weather had been cool and overcast, but at least there had been no wind. After lunch, she went for a walk along the coast. She sat and watched the seals on the rocks. The sun came out. She had felt completely happy. In the late afternoon, she dropped in on Penny, a sculptor we both knew. Penny opened a bottle of wine, even though it was only about five o'clock.

And you drove home? I said.

Rachel laughed. I took the back roads.

When she asked what I'd been up to, I told her I had spent the morning in the prison. There was a silence on the other end.

It's all right, I said. They let me out again.

I thought she would find that funny, but she didn't.

What were you doing there? she said.

I went to see Gino.

Gino?

Gabriella's son.

Oh yes, she said. Isn't he the one who's always getting into trouble?

He's been sentenced to seven years. I told her what little I knew. I've been thinking, I went on quickly. I might visit him while I'm here. Gabriella goes sometimes, and I think Pasquale's been, but otherwise he's got no one.

You'd give him something to look forward to. She paused. You might even do some good.

If I hadn't known Rachel so well, I might have seen her remark as barbed or sarcastic, but that wasn't in her nature. She genuinely believed that I could be of service, and it was in my interest to live up to that belief, since it meant that I was worthy of her forgiveness.

Later, when the phone call was over, I climbed the stairs to my study. Resting on the easel was my Mexican dream painting. Though I had started it two years before, I still had no idea how to convey a man who has the power to kill people with a single glance. If I kept working on the background, perhaps something would occur to me. As I reached for a brush, my thoughts turned to Gino. After I had been with him for about an hour, he went quiet and passed the flat of one hand over the table, a curious gesture that reminded me of someone wiping a hole in the condensation on a window, then he told me that he had a confession to make.

A confession? I said.

His face seemed older suddenly, as if the future had rushed into it.

When I told you that things improved between me and my father, he said, I was lying.

I had no idea what he was referring to.

The week of his funeral, he went on, I came to see you, remember? You asked me if we'd got on better towards the end, and I told you that I'd talked to him not long before he died. I told you that we sat on the sofa in the kitchen and shared a beer. I said that he was proud of me, maybe for the first time ever. Eyes still lowered, he was picking at the surface of the table with one finger. It never happened. I made the whole thing up.

I found myself nodding. The news didn't surprise me as much as he seemed to think it ought to.

Did you realize? he asked.

Not exactly, I said. Though it did sound a bit too good to be true.

I wanted it to be true, he said. For me, obviously—but also for you. I didn't want you to think that he died without us sorting out our differences. But I'm afraid that's how it was. At last, he lifted his eyes to mine. I feel bad about it, Harry. I shouldn't have lied to you.

You did what you did, I said. It doesn't matter.

Not long afterwards, the PA crackled, then let out a squeal of feedback. Visiting hours were about to end.

Adjusting his hoodie, Gino stood up. Do you hate me now?

No, I said. I don't hate you.

I cleaned my brush with turpentine, then I went out through the double doors and onto the balcony. In front of me the ground fell steeply away. A warm wind that came from Africa swirled up from below. In Abruzzo, the wind had a name, but I had forgotten it. I gripped the slender railing and looked out over the drop. On distant mountain ridges, the lights of villages winked and glittered. I thought of Gino in his prison cell. Four walls, no view. *Do you hate me now?* Just then, I sensed a shift or movement in the darkness, and a huge hawk floated past, no more than fifteen feet away. Soaring on the air currents, it remained quite motionless, its wings spread wide, as it flew towards the head of the valley.

The following Thursday, when I sat down with Gino, I told him I had brought him some *ventricina*, a local cured meat that he liked, and also a whole *caciocavallo*, his favorite cheese. The staff on duty at the gates had held on to the food—it needed to be checked—but hopefully they would give it to him later, when I had gone. He thanked me, but seemed nervous or distracted, one of his legs jiggling beneath the table. He wouldn't look at me. His gaze was directed elsewhere, first at the murals, then at the bottle of Coke that was on the table, close to his left hand.

I asked him if he was all right. He said he was fine.

His leg was still jiggling.

How's everyone? he asked. How's Pasquale?

I told him I had helped Pasquale with the *vendemmia* the previous weekend. We had picked the Montepulciano grapes from Alberto's vineyard in the valley. There had been half a dozen of us. Alberto's sons. Pasquale's friend from Naples, Salvatore. It had been hot, almost thirty degrees, but we worked hard and came away with two full tractor loads.

Pasquale must be pleased, Gino said.

He is, I said. You know Pasquà. Nothing matters more to him than wine.

Gino unscrewed the plastic top on his bottle of

Coke and drank a few gulps, then he screwed the top back on. Are you doing any painting?

Remember the Mexican one?

He nodded. The man who kills people just by looking. You think you'll manage it this time, to paint his eyes?

I don't know. I think it might be beyond me.

You'll get there, Harry. You're a good artist. He took another gulp of Coke, then glanced round at the murals. Maybe we should put you to work in here. You could certainly improve on these.

I smiled. It was probably only inmates who were called upon to decorate the walls.

Switching subjects again, Gino asked about Rachel, and I started telling him about her house in Wales. It stood on a crossroads, I said, about three miles from the sea. At the back, she had a long garden that she had turned into a wildflower meadow and a view of a mountain that had once been a volcano. Inside, there was a wood-burning stove, and a crog loft, which was like a kind of mezzanine, looking down into the living room, and when the rain came, as it often did, even in the summer, it fell on the skylight above the bed, a comforting sound if you were drifting off to sleep or if you woke in the middle of the night. She had her favorite walks, to the ruined village at the foot of the mountain, its old stone houses wrapped in ivy and brambles, or out along the coast, where she could watch the seals and the cormorants. Though the sea was cold, she would swim in the small bay near the lifeboat station. Later, she would stop at the Tŷ Coch, a pub that was built right at the water's edge. She would have something to warm her up—a coffee or a ginger wine—then she would make her way back along the beach, to where her car was parked. Gino seemed to relish my descriptions. Was it because they removed him from where he was and put him somewhere different, not back in the world that he had forfeited, but in another world, one that he could only begin to imagine? Maybe. At the same time, I detected an impatience or a longing, as if what I was telling him wasn't quite what he was after.

That's why she hardly ever comes to Italy, I told him. She already has everything she needs.

Except for you.

Oh, she can do without me—for a month or two, anyway. And we talk most days, on the phone.

Is that really why she doesn't come?

He finished his Coke and screwed the top back on the empty bottle.

There's something I've never understood, he went on quickly. After all the bad things you did, why did she agree to take you back?

I don't usually talk about that, I said.

He fixed me with a plaintive look, and given how open and candid he had always been with me, it didn't seem fair to deny him.

I've often asked myself the same question, I went on, and honestly, Gino, I'm not sure that I know the answer.

My gaze drifted to the far end of the room, the bars on the windows dividing the sky into dozens of small blue squares. After several years apart, I started thinking about Rachel incessantly. I missed her in my head, but also in my belly. In my guts. The feeling was a lot like hunger. Without her, I didn't think that I'd be able to go on. I flew back to the UK. To my surprise, she was willing to meet. We talked until dawn, and I pleaded with her, and both of us cried, though not at the same time, and not for the same reason. It wasn't for her to dredge up my wrongdoing, she told me, and she wasn't about to ask me to repent, because saying sorry is like going backwards, and she only cared about going forwards—and besides, she said, people always say they're sorry. Those words come too easily, and have no weight. She could only have me back if I was true to her from now on, for as long as we both lived.

I looked at Gino, who was still waiting for me to speak. Somehow, she was able to forgive me, I said. Somehow, she found it in her heart.

She must be an exceptional woman, he said, to give you another chance like that.

She is. I paused. In her shoes, I don't think I would have been so generous.

You're lucky, Harry. Really.

Later, as I drove down the Adriatica, towards Vasto, I realized that it was luck that Gino wanted to hear about. And he wanted that luck for himself. He needed it. He was hoping it was like a skill or a gift—something that might rub off on him, something that could be acquired. But I didn't think that luck had played much of a part in Rachel's decision to take me back. It had more to do with being older. Not calmer, necessarily, or more stoical, or even less demanding. Just older. There's a good deal behind you, and not so much ahead, which means that whatever's coming has pressure on it, and is precious. Perhaps that makes forgiveness easier, or more available as an option. I don't know. In any case, it wasn't a thought that Gino would find very reassuring. He wasn't even thirty yet, and nor was Franca.


That Sunday, after mass, Gabriella was waiting for me when I left the church. She wanted to know if my wife would be joining me this autumn. I told her that Rachel couldn't come, as she was caring for her ailing mother. It wasn't true—Rachel's mother was surprisingly fit for a woman of eighty-six—but it was the kind of lie that Gabriella would believe, and it was simpler than trying to explain why Rachel would rather be in Wales, which was something Gabriella would find hard to understand. In her book, a wife's place was with her husband.

She asked if I had been to see Gino.

I've been twice, I told her.

How did he seem?

About as good as you could expect, given the circumstances. He didn't mention Franca, though. I found that strange.

She hasn't visited, Gabriella said.

Not at all?

Not even once.

Gabriella looked away from me, her copper-tinted hair synthetic in the daylight. On the first floor of the apartment building opposite was a balcony that was brightened by pots of red geraniums. A woman I had never seen before was hanging out her washing.

She's moved out of the house, Gabriella told me.

La Peschiera?

Gabriella nodded.

I thought she loved it there, I said.

I thought so too. Gabriella stared at me, as if the whole subject was utterly unfathomable.

Where is she living now? I asked.

How would I know? Gabriella said through gritted teeth. No one tells me anything.

Muttering to herself, she turned away from me, towards her car. She almost hit the back of a parked van as she drove out of the piazza.


On my third visit to Torre Sinello, in mid-October, I learned that Gino had been assigned to the workshop, where he was making bed linen for prisons all over Italy. Operating a sewing machine might be boring, he told me, but it was better than sitting in your cell. There was more light, more air. And he was being paid a small salary as well. He could buy cigarettes. Soft drinks. His head dropped, and his shoulders began to shake.

What's the matter, Gino? I said.

It was a while before he answered, and when he spoke he kept his head lowered.

I was thinking about the present you gave us when we got married. Those lovely sheets. He looked up at me, his eyelashes wet. I haven't seen Franca since I went to trial. I haven't even heard from her. No phone call, no letter. Nothing. Once again, he passed the flat of his hand over the surface of the table, but this time the gesture was slow and tremulous, as if something had come between him and the world, and he was powerless to change it. It's been almost five months, he went on. I think she's given up on me.

I'm sure that's not true, I said.

You're sure? His voice was abrasive suddenly. How can you be sure? Have you seen her?

I'm sorry. You're right. I have no idea.

He rubbed his face with both hands, then he leaned forwards, over the table. It's me who should be sorry. I shouldn't have bitten your head off like that.

It's okay, I said. I understand.

We sat in silence, looking in different directions. I was wondering if it had been wise of me to get involved. Perhaps I had an exaggerated sense of my own capabilities, my own importance. What if I was doing more harm than good? It would hardly be the first time.

Harry, Gino said eventually, I have a favor to ask.

Of course, I said. Anything.

Would you go and talk to her? He looked at me with a kind of yearning. You could put in a good word for me. She'll listen to you, I know she will. She has always had the greatest respect for you.

I hesitated. When I thought about Franca, I realized that I scarcely knew her at all.

See that? Gino was pointing at the mural behind me. Sometimes I think I see her standing there, next to that streetlamp. She's facing away from me. I call her name—I call and call—but she never answers. I only ever see the back of her. It's almost worse than not seeing her at all. He reached across the table and gripped my wrist. If you were to speak to her, Harry, she might change her mind. She might even turn around and look at me. He glanced down, then up again. Please. I don't know who else to ask.

Okay, I said. I'll try.

Thank you. His grip tightened, then relaxed, and he sat back. God. Thank you so much.

I can't promise anything.

Of course not. His eyes filled with tears again. You're a real friend, Harry. What would I do without you?

That same evening, I walked up the hill to Franca's parents' apartment and rang the bell. Marcello came to the door in a soiled yellow polo shirt. He hadn't shaved, and he smelled of crushed grapes and stale sweat. As he led me into the kitchen, he told me that Silvana was away for a few days, visiting her father in Teramo. He was taking advantage of her absence to do some work in his *cantina*.

I sat beneath a shadeless light bulb while he poured me a glass of his own red wine. Sangiovese from two years ago, he said. Though I wasn't hungry, he cut several slices of bread, cold meat, and cheese, and arranged them on a wooden board in the middle of the table. We talked about the recent hot weather, and the sugar content of the grapes, and also about the number of houses in the village that were being bought up by foreigners.

Soon there'll be more of you than there are of us, Marcello joked.

There was a lull.

I've seen Gino, I said.

Something tightened or twisted in Marcello's face, and he looked down into his glass. Yes, I heard.

It must be hard for Franca.

It's hard for all of us.

I reached out and took a wedge of cheese. They say she's left La Peschiera.

Marcello's eyes darted towards me. Who told you that?

Gabriella.

He nodded to himself, then drank. She's moved to Lanciano. Antonella helped her find a place.

I thought she liked it in the country.

Too many memories. He drank again. And she can't live out there on her own, not with a small child. It's just not practical.

I murmured that I could see his point.

Gino, he said, then slowly shook his head. This time he went too far. I tried to warn her, as any father would. She didn't listen.

You don't think she'll give him one more chance?

He's in Torre Sinello for seven years. If he's lucky, he'll be out in five. What's she supposed to do? Wait?

I swirled the wine in my glass.

If she loved him, I said.

Marcello let out an exasperated sigh. She's not prepared to deal with the madness anymore. She's had enough. He rose from the table and moved over to the window. There was no view, only the side wall of the apartment block next door. Don't you remember the time he threatencd to cut his father's throat? He was down in the piazza with a knife, screaming his head off. Gabriella was beside herself.

I heard about it, I said. I wasn't here.

When they got married, Marcello went on, I gave him the benefit of the doubt. I thought he'd changed. He hadn't, though.

All the same, I'd like to talk to Franca.

He gave a shrug that had an edge of disdain or disgust in it—not for me, but for the idea.

Talk to her, he said. No one's going to stop you.

Do you have her new address?

He found an old envelope and scribbled on it, then he handed it to me. Filling his glass again, he pushed the bottle across the table towards me.

I thanked him, but said I had to be going.


Though I had all the information I needed—along with Franca's new address, Marcello had given me her phone number—I found myself incapable of acting on it. Instead, I worked with Pasquale, helping him to put the latest haul of Montepulciano grapes through the winepresses. I drove to *Rusi Isaia* in Vasto and bought a new fridge. I walked to the neighboring village of Furci and back, which took most of a day. What I couldn't seem to do was to make good on my promise to Gino.

On Monday evening, I was still delaying things when Rachel called to tell me that she had slipped on wet leaves in the street and fallen over. She had fractured her left wrist. They had taken her to the hospital in Bangor. It wasn't serious, she said. Just a nuisance, that's all. Without thinking, I offered to fly back earlier than planned. Are you sure? she said. I know how much you love it there. Of course I'm sure, I said. I'll come home as soon as I can. After bringing my flight forward to the following weekend, I realized that I would only be able to visit Gino one more time.

This unexpected alteration in my plans broke the deadlock. On Tuesday morning, I set off for Lanciano. I could have phoned ahead, but I was worried that Franca might refuse to see me. I decided, on balance, that it would be better to arrive unannounced. After passing a ceramics workshop on the outskirts of Lanciano, I followed the road round to the right, then took a turning up a small incline, into an area populated by modern, pastel-colored apartment buildings. I found the address without too much trouble. Franca lived on the ground floor, at the back. A persimmon tree grew in the corner of the yard, its orange fruit glowing in the autumn sunlight. Nearby, under a lean-to, was a dirt bike, a stack of roof tiles, and half a dozen old toilet cisterns.

When Franca answered the door, her surprise only lasted a second or two. It was replaced by cautiousness, or even apprehension. We hadn't seen each other in almost eighteen months, and it was possible that she had forgotten I existed. It was also possible that she hadn't wanted to be tracked down, least of all by people from Caracciolo. I had the distinct impression, even in those awkward first moments, that she had embarked on a life that was entirely new.

Harry, she said.

I made up a story about having an appointment at my bank that morning. Since I happened to be in Lanciano, I had decided to look her up.

She said it was nice of me to take the trouble.

Well, we're old friends, aren't we, I said. I ran into your father the other day. He told me that you'd moved up here.

I haven't been here long. Only a couple of months.

She showed me into a small kitchen. A marble-topped table in the middle, with three chairs and a high chair. Copper pans hanging from hooks. A window with a view of the persimmon tree. The room was neat and orderly, though sparsely furnished. There were no luxuries, nothing unnecessary or excessive.

Would you like a coffee? she asked.

I'd love one, I said.

Her hair was shorter than I remembered, barely shoulder-length, and she was wearing a green T-shirt and a short brown skirt. You would never have guessed that she had had a child. She looked too young.

Loosening my coat, I took a seat at the table.

Elio was asleep, she told me as she lit the gas under the coffeepot, but he would wake soon.

I asked how he was.

He'll be two in December, she said.

She put a cup of coffee in front of me, then stood back with her arms folded. I saw that wariness came naturally to her. It was already there in the steady, narrow eyes, and in the sharp planes of her face. She had always had something of the fox about her. That sudden, absolute stillness, that pricking of the ears. That readiness to flee.

Sit with me, I said. Please. I won't be staying long.

Reluctantly, she pulled out a chair.

I asked what life was like in Lanciano. She told me it was a proper town. There was lots to do. Even though she had a child, she had managed to make friends. She had also found a part-time job in an opticians'. Her aunt Antonella lived nearby. Antonella looked after Elio while she was out at work. It was a good arrangement.

I was about to mention Gino when a cry came from the next room.

Her face brightened. Elio.

Seconds later, she appeared in the kitchen doorway with her son in her arms. The wide, violet-colored eyes, the dark hair. The flawless skin. He looked as extraordinary as ever. Perhaps even more so.

This is Harry, she told him.

Hello Elio, I said.

She settled him on a rug in the corner with his toys, then she returned to the table and sat down. I could put it off no longer.

I've been to the prison, I said.

She stood up again immediately and went to the sink. Turning on the tap, she began to wash her hands, though I didn't think they needed washing. A vein showed in the back of her right knee. I watched as she reached sideways for a tea towel. She dried her hands with an attentiveness that suggested it was a pleasure or an extravagance, and should not be hurried.

Elio tottered towards me, holding out a wooden Pinocchio. I took it from him. After regarding me with an expression that was intent and grave, as if he had given me something far more important than a toy, as if, in accepting the Pinocchio, I had taken part in a ceremonial act, or made some kind of promise or commitment, he went back to the rug in the corner. I stared at the figure in my hand—the long nose, the pointed hat. What was I being told? Not to lie? I glanced at Franca, but she still had her back to me.

He misses you terribly, I told her. He wishes he could see you.

Maybe he should have thought of that, she said, before he tried to burn down someone's house.

She turned from the sink, and as she stood there, gripping the edge of the work surface with both hands, the inside of her elbows facing outwards, an unnerving, almost primal emanation came from her, something you could call radiance, perhaps, or even beauty, and suddenly it made perfect sense to me that Gino had behaved as he had. You might almost say that she had driven him to it—except that would have been unfair, since I didn't think that she was in control of the effect she had on him, or on other people, for that matter. She might actually have been unaware of it. For that reason she was dangerous, and also innocent.

His obsession with that man, I told her, it's a measure of how much he loves you, don't you see?

That's not love, she said. That's something else.

All the light in the room was coming from the window behind her. My face felt exposed, while hers remained unreadable, in shadow.

I don't know if I ever told you this, Harry, she went on, but I gave myself to him completely. I told him I was his, and only his—words I'd never said before, to anyone. Somehow—I don't know—it was too much for him. He couldn't trust it. Maybe it even frightened him.

Maybe he would trust it now, I said. Maybe he has learned. I leaned over and put the Pinocchio on the floor, not far from Elio.

No, she said. He'll never learn. I know that now.

How can you be sure?

Because he had so many chances. She pushed her hair back from her forehead with the spread fingers of one hand. Once, when we were renovating La Peschiera, she went on, we fell asleep in the afternoon, and I dreamt that he was walking away from me. I called after him, but he didn't hear me. He just kept walking. When we woke up, I told him about the dream. That wasn't something he would ever do, he said. He would never walk away from me like that. But that's exactly what he did. Lowering her head, she removed a piece of lint from her T-shirt, then she looked up again. He broke something. It's over.

There's really no way back for him?

She stared at me hard, as if, in persisting, I was willfully misunderstanding a situation that ought to have been clear to me, then she looked off into the corner of the room.

The thought crossed my mind, as I watched her, that she might have met somebody else, but I dismissed it straight away. It wasn't in character for her to have betrayed Gino, even though his actions had been so extreme as to have him locked up. She had always had a stubborn, steadfast quality—the very opposite of faithlessness. In fact, that was why I hadn't believed Gino when he said he suspected her of seeing Pierozzi behind his back.

I looked down into my coffee cup. It was empty.

She asked if I would like some more.

No, I said. Thank you.

I lifted my eyes to the window. It hadn't gone the way I'd hoped it would. There was a pitiless certainty about her which I hadn't anticipated, and which neutralized or nullified everything I said. I had been forced to exaggerate. *Maybe he has learned.* That was a half-truth at best—and if I didn't believe it, why should she?

I should go, I said.

She showed me to the door with Elio in her arms. He was pointing past me, at the dirt bike parked under the lean-to. She set him down. We stood and watched as he staggered off across the yard.

I don't hold it against you, she said, coming here and pleading for him. I know you mean well. But he's on his own now.

I thought of Gino in the Visitors' Room, eyes cast down, the sleeves on his hoodie covering the fact that he had cut himself. His hand moving over the table, as if looking for a way out. A hand that seemed tentative. Blind. The tall gray streetlamp, and Franca standing next to it, facing down the dusty track. Facing away from him—forever.

I asked if she would allow him to see Elio.

Maybe. I don't know. She folded her arms. We'll deal with that when the time comes.

I turned away, then I turned back again. What he accused you of, it was ridiculous, wasn't it. He was just imagining things.

Her eyes flared. You're really asking me that?

Sorry, I said. It's none of my business.

I waved goodbye to Elio, who was sitting by the bike, then I walked back to my car.

On the third Thursday in October, I drove to the prison, knowing that it would be my last visit for a while. When I left the village, the sun was shining, but as I approached the Adriatica half an hour later, a wall of mist or fog loomed in front of me, and the temperature dropped by almost ten degrees. Trucks surged out of the white haze, headlights blazing. To the left, beyond the vineyards, the sea was invisible.

As I registered at the gatehouse, I found myself thinking about Franca's innocence. It wasn't that she had done anything she shouldn't have. She had been loyal to Gino, and she had every right to think of herself as wronged, and also blameless. Whatever quality it was that had drawn him to her had led him to doubt her too.

That same quality had prompted me to ask a question that I had never meant to ask. I had upset her. It seemed unlikely that she would want to see me again.

When Gino sat down at the table in the Visitors' Room, he wasted no time in getting to the point. Did you talk to her?

I nodded. Yes.

And Elio? He was there too?

He's well.

Where did you meet? he asked. Did you drive out to La Peschiera?

Gino, I said, they don't live there anymore.

He stared at me, mouth open. I had assumed that Gabriella would have told him. Apparently not.

They've moved to Lanciano, I went on. Near Franca's aunt.

Lanciano?

This wasn't something he had expected. Also, the town had bad associations for him. When he was younger—nineteen or twenty—he had been removed to a psychiatric unit in Lanciano against his will.

She's renting a ground-floor apartment, I told him, on the outskirts of the town.

I repeated what Franca had said to me in her small, neat kitchen, and what she had said afterwards, in the yard, as I was leaving. I chose not to mention my feeling that she had embarked on a new life, a life in which he had no place. That wouldn't have been fair on him.

Even so, he fell still at the table, and his lips suddenly looked pale, as if all the blood had been drawn deep into his body. In his face, I saw a gauntness that I had seen in other prisoners. Perhaps everyone who has been locked away begins, after a while, to have a dehydrated look. Freedom is like moisture. Without it, we dry up, turning into shells or husks of the people we once were.

At last, he spoke. *She said that?*

I shifted on my chair. What?

*He broke something.*

Yes.

He put both elbows on the table and covered his face with his hands. His nails were bitten, and one of his knuckles was badly grazed.

I'm sorry, Gino, I said. I tried my best.

He stayed in that position for a long time—two minutes maybe, or even three—and when he finally took his hands away from his face, his eyes were bloodshot.

And what do you think, Harry? he said slowly, his voice uncertain. Do you think she means what she says?

You know her much better than I do.

But what do you think?

He wanted to hear my point of view. I came from a different country, a different culture. I might have a more favorable interpretation.

I think she means it, I said, for now.

For now, he said heavily, as if we were talking about an eternity.

I leaned forwards, over the table. What happened is still so recent, I told him. If you give her time, she might change her mind. I was thinking hard, looking not just for reasons but also for the words in which to frame them. In time, I said, she might start missing you. It's not easy to bring up a child on your own. I paused again. After all, she waited for you once before—for years. She could wait for you again.

He nodded, but didn't seem convinced.

Later, as visiting hours were coming to an end, I told him to be patient. Above all, he shouldn't give up. He should never give up.

He sat back. Have you noticed how everything in here is painted green? he said. The doors, the window frames—the metal gates that separate one part of the prison from another?

I nodded.

A few days ago I asked one of the guards why there's so much green. You know what he said? It's the color of hope. Gino smiled blankly, bitterly. It's just a color.

There was nothing I could say to that.

We stood up from the table.

I won't be able to come and see you for a while, I told him.

What do you mean? He looked so dismayed that I realized I should have told him at the beginning, when he first walked in. I should have given him more of a chance to absorb the news.

I have to leave earlier than expected, I said. Problems at home.

He hung his head, as if abandonment was no more or less than he deserved. I'll miss you. I'll miss our conversations.

As we gave each other a hug, I spoke into the air behind his shoulder. I'll be back before you know it.

It wasn't true. I would be gone for months. Who would visit Gino during the long, cold days of winter? Maybe his mother. Maybe nobody. Patience, I thought. Hope. It was easy for me to say. But for someone in his predicament, with too much time on his hands and nothing to sustain him?

Later still, in the prison car park, I sat behind the wheel of my car, not moving. There was a tightness in my stomach, and in my throat. My ears hissed. The rearview mirror showed me a guard tower, the tinted-glass cabin perched at one corner of the perimeter wall. After leaving Franca's apartment on Tuesday, I'd stopped at the ceramics workshop further down the road. I entered an enormous shed, not sure why I was there. Ignoring the array of plates and bowls, I walked through to the back, where a number of figures stood side by side on a low shelf. I was drawn, as if by a mysterious force, to a statue of a man dressed in a green robe, with a wooden club in his left hand. A flame hovered above his head. In less than five minutes, the transaction was complete. A young man carried the statue out to my car. Standing it upright on the back seat, he fastened a seat belt around it to hold it in place. Each time I looked in the rearview mirror on my way home, I saw that I had a passenger, seemingly strapped into the car against his will. St. Jude, patron saint of lost causes.

An ordinary November day in Wales, the mountains wrapped in cloud and mist, rain in the air. In the morning, as always, we drove down to the sea. Leaving the car in the National Trust car park, we climbed the hill to the clubhouse, then started out across the golf course. The plaster had been removed from Rachel's arm, and though her wrist still felt weak she was confident that the break had mended well. We followed the footpath that led to the headland, but there weren't any cormorants or seals on the rocks, only a few gulls, so we doubled back, passing the lifeboat station, then walked on round the coast, towards Porthdinllaen. Once in a while, we would stop at the pub for a drink, but that day we kept moving, past the other buildings in the village, and on into the next bay, which was more enclosed, and stonier, and smelled of rotting seaweed and rust. On the far side of the bay was a white house that stood alone in the shadow of the cliffs. Beyond it was Morfa Nefyn beach, almost two miles long.

The tide was out, and the wet sand gleamed, even though the sun was hidden behind a mass of clouds. It was Rachel's belief that this particular stretch of beach had magical powers. You should try not to think a negative thought, she would tell me, as it would be treated as a wish, and would probably come true. Think only good things, she would say. I was carrying my shoes and socks, as I liked walking close to where the waves broke. Rachel was fifty yards to my right, and a little ahead of me. Her scarlet anorak, her gray-blonde hair.

We were about halfway along the beach when my phone began to ring. It was Pasquale, calling from Abruzzo. This was unheard of. In all the years that I had known Pasquale, I don't think he had ever called, not when I wasn't in the village.

Pasquale, I said, this is a surprise.

I have bad news, he said.

What's happened?

Gino's dead.

I stared out towards the horizon. The sky was dark gray, and the sea below was so eerily flat and opal-colored that it looked ghostly. Small waves whispered against the sand.

He had been found hanging in his cell, Pasquale told me. There was no suspicion of foul play. Though he hadn't left a note, it was being treated as a suicide.

I thought you should know, Pasquale said.

I thanked him for telling me.

We only spoke for about two minutes, and when Pasquale said goodbye I stood quite motionless, aware of the phone in my hand, lifeless as a brick or a stone. I had the sudden, strange urge to hurl it into the water. A breath of wind moved round me in a half circle, testing my clothes.

I sensed Rachel approaching.

I was calling you, she said.

I'm sorry. I didn't hear you. I was still staring out over the calm, pale sea with the phone in my hand, solid and unfeeling.

What is it? she asked.

Gino's dead. He hanged himself. The words tasted bitter as metal in my mouth. I wanted to spit, but didn't.

Hanged himself? Her voice was quiet, shocked.

I nodded. In prison. In his cell.

I'm so sorry, Harry, she said. I know you cared for him.

I didn't care enough.

She murmured something consoling, then she took my arm and we walked on, along the sand. I thought I knew what she was thinking. We needed to move from the place where the phone call had happened. If I stayed there too long, the wrong emotions would root themselves in me, emotions like despair and melancholy.

We reached the slipway and turned inland, passing a row of cottages with white facades and pale-blue doors and window frames. They stood right on the beach, facing the sea. A concrete wall had been built in front of them to protect against storm surges.

I should never have told him about Franca, I said. I should have pretended not to have seen her. I could have said that I drove out to La Peschiera, only to find that the house was empty. I could have said that Marcello refused to tell me where she was. I could have told him that I hadn't had the time to look for her. I swallowed hard. Better still, I shouldn't have gone to see her in the first place. I should have kept out of it.

Rachel argued that it would have made no difference, not in the end. If you hadn't told him, she said, someone else would have.

I wasn't sensitive enough—

You were a good friend to him, Harry. You did everything you could.

But she didn't know, not really. She had no real knowledge of the people involved. She wasn't close enough to them. In spite of what she had said, I blamed myself. There were things I could have done differently, things I needn't have done at all, instead of which I'd waded in, convinced that I was being useful. What was it about me? Why did I cause such chaos? In my mind's eye, I saw St. Jude again—the downturned mouth, that tongue of pentecostal flame above his head. At last I understood why I had bought the statue. It would serve to remind me of my shortcomings—all that I had failed to accomplish.

Near the top of the hill, we turned along a mud path that led between high hedges. The montbretias that grew at the edge of the path had died back, their fiery orange flowers extinguished. By now, the sky was darker still, but it was only when we were in the car park, a few yards from our car, that the rain came sweeping across the fields. In a hurry suddenly, we pulled the doors open and scrambled in.

Rachel looked at me as we sat there, breathing hard.

We were lucky, weren't we, she said.

That evening, as I pulled a chair up to the wood-burning stove, the rain loud against the skylight, my thoughts took an unexpected turn. I found myself going back over the last conversation that I'd had with Marcello. In retrospect, it surprised me that he had shared Franca's contact details so willingly. Surely, if he approved of her separation from Gino, as he seemed to, he should have kept me—Gino's friend—from knowing where she lived? Wouldn't it have made more sense for him to try to prevent a dialogue developing, even if it was through an intermediary? He could have refused to tell me where she was, claiming that she was starting over, and that she was entitled to some privacy. I began to wonder whether he might have had a hidden agenda. Had he known what Franca would say to me? And had he also known that I would pass on what she had said to Gino? Furthermore, had he understood how fragile Gino was, and what effect those words were likely to have? It was possible that he had used me to rid his daughter of her inconvenient husband. Perhaps it had been his intention all along to undermine—or even to destroy—his troubled son-in-law.

Still gazing at the fire, I leaned back in my chair.

I had always thought of the ambulance driver as a genial character. He had his own catchphrases, but when you said something funny yourself there would be a delay before he reacted, and his laughter, when it finally happened, seemed to come as something of a shock to him, as if he didn't expect jokes from other people, or as if he was astonished to be laughing at all. At times like that, I thought him foolish, a little slow—but still someone I was happy to sit down with. What if there was another side to him, though? What if he was more cunning—or more venal—than I had realized? After all, hadn't he been close to Pierozzi once?


Eight months later, in the middle of July, I returned to Abruzzo. Rachel stayed behind in Wales, as extreme heat didn't agree with her. She would join me in September, perhaps, if I was still there, or we could always go together next time, in the spring. I had been back for about two weeks when I drove up to Lanciano. My appointment with the bank was at ten o'clock. An hour later, once all my business had been concluded, I walked into the *centro storico*, a maze of narrow, cobbled streets and passageways, and grand, crumbling apartment buildings with wrought-iron balconies and metal-studded doors. I had nothing particular in mind. I was simply wandering—aimlessly, but with a pleasure that was both intense and subdued. You take one turning, then another. You open yourself to chance discoveries. You're adrift, but never lost. It felt good to be plunged into the shade, which was cool and damp, the sky squeezed into a skinny, jagged strip of blue by the tallness of the houses that surrounded me. At some point, if I found a place that was to my liking, I would stop for lunch. Through an entrance, and on into a dark interior. A pasta dish, some bread. A glass of local wine.

That morning, I ventured north of the cathedral, into a part of the old town that I wasn't familiar with. Before too long, I found myself in a modest, tiled piazza with a drinking fountain at one end and a row of trees on either side, and there, only yards away, was a young woman with a little boy. I recognized them immediately.

Franca and Elio.

Franca was facing away from me. Her eyes were on her son, who was chasing a pigeon. They were the only people in the piazza, apart from a man in a white vest and blue work trousers who was sweeping up the seedpods that had fallen from a tree in the far corner. I had come to a standstill, beneath a shop's striped awning. Should I go over and greet her, or should I back away, into the alley, and leave her be? I could pretend that I hadn't seen her, that I was never there. As I hesitated, she seemed to sense me behind her, and she sent a glance in my direction, her eyes narrowed, her chin close to her left shoulder. The look was typical of her—provocative and challenging, but also wary.

I moved towards her and said hello.

She smiled faintly. Her hair had grown, falling past her collarbone. Though it was the height of summer, her face was pale.

Were you at the bank again? she said.

I smiled back. As a matter of fact, I was. Renewing my house insurance. I made a gesture that suggested necessity, and also boredom. How are you, Franca?

I'm well.

I looked at Elio, who was still running after the pigeon. He's growing fast.

Yes, she said. He's tall for his age.

How old is he now?

Two and a half.

All her furtiveness disappeared when she looked at her son. All her apprehension. She seemed like a different person, open and serene.

It suits you, I said, being a mother.

Thank you, she said.

We were both quiet, watching Elio, who had stopped in front of the drinking fountain. He was reaching up and trying to press the knob that released the water.

It was terrible, I said, what happened to Gino.

Something shook Franca's slender body, as if a tremor or a spasm had gone through her, and she sank down onto a nearby bench. I went and sat beside her. We were in the shade of a tree whose leaves were such a dark purple that they were almost black.

I'm sorry, I said. Perhaps I shouldn't have brought it up.

It's all right, she said. I know it was months ago, but I'm still not over it.

Of course not.

I was so shocked. Tears were spilling down her cheeks, but she didn't lower her head or cover her face. The weird thing is, I feel responsible. As if I did it to him myself.

I was about to say that I also felt responsible when Elio came over.

Mamma?

She touched the back of her hand to one eye, then the other.

I'm fine, darling, she said. You go and play.

But he had placed a hand on her knee, and he was studying her intently. His expression was concerned, but also luminous, somehow, the dark hair falling across his forehead, his eyes a mauve-gray that reminded me, curiously, of the slate that Wales is famous for, and I remembered the stories about complete strangers arriving outside their house in the country at all hours of the day and night, and suddenly I understood why those people might have gone out of their way to spend a few moments in his presence. I also remembered something that I had said to Gino when he appeared on my doorstep after an argument with Franca and sat at the kitchen table and talked about his son—how beautiful the child was, and how he was worried that he might not be the father. He's the beauty inside you that you didn't know about, I told him. The beauty that you couldn't see. And there it is, I thought, right in front of me. You could almost say that Gino was still with us, in the world. The best part of him, at least.

Franca was pointing. The pigeon's back.

One hand still resting on her knee, Elio looked where she was looking. Pigeon, he cried, and then he turned and scampered after it.

Franca smiled through her tears. I wonder if Gino chased pigeons when he was little.

I gave a start.

What is it? she said.

Nothing, I said. Someone must have walked over my grave.

She gave me an odd look. Clearly, she had never heard the phrase before.

It's what English people say, I told her, when they shudder for no reason.

Except in this case, of course, there had been a reason. In her mind, Elio's father was Gino, not Pierozzi—there was no doubt about it—and she had just let that be known. Possibly without meaning to, or even being aware of it, she had answered the question I had asked the previous year, in the yard outside her apartment.

Leaning forwards, my elbows on my knees, I watched the boy run after the pigeon. When the pigeon sensed him approaching, it would take off with a clatter of its wings, and he would stand still, gazing after it with a rapt expression on his face, and then the pigeon would land again, in another part of the piazza, as if it had forgotten all about the boy, as if those few seconds in the air had erased its memory. And he would go after it once more. It kept happening, over and over. It was like a ritual. A dance. The two of them seemed to be illustrating some kind of truth or wisdom.

I loved him, you know, Franca said.

I looked at her over my shoulder. Her face seemed set against a future that was likely to be difficult.

I know you did, I said.

I really did. I still do. But maybe, for him, that wasn't enough. Or maybe it was too much. She paused. Sometimes love isn't where you belong. You belong somewhere else.

I wasn't sure I understood, but I said nothing.

She sniffed twice, quickly. I don't know what else I could have done.

I leaned back again. You couldn't have done anything, I told her. No one could. The bench's horizontal wooden bars felt hard against my spine. You were happy for a while, though, weren't you.

Very happy.

Maybe it's best just to think of that.

I can't. It's too upsetting. She took hold of her long hair in both hands and twisted it, then dropped it behind her back. To tell you the truth, I'd rather not think of him at all.

In that case, I said, do what's best for you and Elio.

She nodded.

For a while, neither of us spoke.

Tiring of the pigeon, Elio came and stood at his mother's shoulder. Like us, he seemed thoughtful. In the distance, the man was still sweeping up seedpods and leaves, his brushstrokes so regular that they could have been used to measure time or send someone to sleep.

Well, I said at last, standing up from the bench, I should probably go and find some lunch.

Franca rose to her feet and gestured towards the far corner of the piazza. There's a place down that street. I don't remember what it's called. The food is good, though, and you won't pay much.

Thank you, I said. I'll give it a try.

Goodbye, Harry.

Goodbye.

As I looked at her and smiled, I had the feeling that this leave-taking was final, and that I would never see her again, even though I would have to come to Lanciano from time to time, on business.

We embraced quickly, and then I ruffled Elio's hair and turned away. The man with the broom glanced at me as I walked past, but didn't stop his work.

When I reached the far side of the piazza, I looked back over my shoulder. Franca and Elio were gone. For a few moments, I felt that I had imagined the whole thing. Our chance meeting had a dream's rapidly evaporating quality, vivid yet ephemeral. The boy chasing the pigeon, the man sweeping. The young woman on the bench, in tears. What Franca had said seemed dreamlike too, as if the words had come through her, not from her. *Sometimes love isn't where you belong.* I still wasn't sure what she meant by that. I shook my head, then, hungry suddenly, I set off down the alley, moving from bright sunlight into shadow.

## ACKNOWLEDGMENTS

Thank you to my early readers: Liz Calder, Rory Farquhar-Thomson, and Katharine Norbury, all of whom gave me notes on the manuscript. And special thanks to Laura Revelli Beaumont, who read at least two different versions of the book.

Thank you to Giuseppe Rossi, and the staff at the Casa di Lavoro in Vasto.

Thank you to Don Silvio Santovito in Casalbordino.

Thank you to Samuel Thomson.

Thank you to Ian Galea and Giada Middei, and the staff at the Albergo Diffuso Locanda Specchio di Diana in Nemi.

Thank you to everyone who works at the Portobello service station on the Adriatica, near Casalbordino.

Finally, a huge thank you to the people of San Buono—especially to Don Pieralbert D'Alessandro, Giovanni Di Noro and Teresa Delle Donne, and Rita and Vittorio Sambrotta.

**Rupert Thomson** is the author of more than a dozen critically acclaimed novels, including *Barcelona Dreaming*, which was short-listed for the Edward Stanford Fiction with a Sense of Place Award, *Never Anyone But You*, which was short-listed for the American Library in Paris Book Award, *Death of a Murderer*, which was short-listed for the Costa Novel of the Year Award, and *The Insult*, which was short-listed for the Guardian Fiction Prize and selected by David Bowie as one of his 100 Must-Read Books of All Time. His memoir, *This Party's Got to Stop*, was named the Writers' Guild Non-Fiction Book of the Year. He is a Fellow of the Royal Society of Literature and lives in London.